Mistress Memoirs

Mistress

Memoirs

Lorraine Elzia

Peace In The Storm Publishing, LLC

Acknowledgments

Even the sun needs help in order to shine. Our best qualities are enhanced with a little love and help from family and friends. They encourage us, support us and keep us grounded so that others are able to see our rays.

I give birth to *Mistress Memoirs* after a lot of Prenatal Care from the hands of those around me. Through the efforts of all that have touched my life in one way or another, Mistress Memoirs was able to grow inside me and I was able to give it life.

To my husband I thank you for allowing me to be me; strengths and flaws included, and for giving me unconditional love and support in all that I do.

To my mother and my sons, I thank you for putting up with my ways when I was in "my zone" and loving me in spite of.

To my sisters, either by blood or by choice; Rrachelle, Lisa, Stephanie and Crystal, I thank each of you for constantly reminding me that I couldn't just talk about it; I had to "be about it."

I give thanks to Essentially Women Writing Group and KIRS (Keeping it Real Sisters) for always encouraging me that I had a voice that needed to be heard in only the way that I could say it.

I give thanks to Jacqueline Moore and Sharon Gray for being sounding boards for me when I was in doubt. They allowed me to vent; then gave me the tough love I needed to push pass my pity party and get closer to my goal.

Much love is given to all my online friends who endured my ADQ's (A Deeva Quickies), my endless ranting and raving emails, and who planted the initial seed in me that writing was my forte. I love each and every one of you.

Special thanks to the Court Reporters who allowed me to pick their brains concerning their profession.

I also give thanks to each of the Anthologies that I am in or have been a part of. It was the acceptance of my submissions to them that gave me the confidence I needed to try and write a book of my own. Thanks for giving me an inch so that I could run with it and take a mile.

Much love, honor, respect and thanks to Elissa Gabrielle and Peace in the Storm publishing for all the mentoring, support and guidance that made this book possible. Elissa has been a gift from God in my life, and I thank her for seeing something in my writing that made her give me this opportunity.

Finally, I thank my Lord and Savior, Jesus Christ. God could have taken me from this place a few years ago, but He chose not to. He told me that He had decided to let me hang around for a while because I had a story or two to tell the world; I had a purpose to fulfill. He showed me that I am blessed and highly favored, and I thank Him for loving me enough to spare me and for His grace and continuous mercy over my life.

If I have forgotten anyone, please chalk it up to my head and not my heart. There have been so many of you that have impacted my life, and my heart has been filled with so much love and support that my head is overwhelmed, yet I thank you all as well.

Lorraine *(A Deeva)* Elzia

Praise for

Mistress Memoirs

"There are times when we are blessed with an incredible talent that far outshines and outweighs the status quo. Lorraine Elzia is a breath of fresh air whose brilliant gift of the written word will dazzle and delight. Lorraine Elzia is one to watch out for as she brings the sizzle and raises the bar in this delicious and decadent look into the mind of the other woman."

~Elissa Gabrielle, President & CEO
Peace In The Storm Publishing

"Author Lorraine Elzia has written a captivating tale of 'cat and mouse' that commands your attention from the first word to the last syllable. "Mistress Memoirs" should be on every woman's reading list as this author, through her memorable characters, shows how easy it is to become your own worst nightmare...a mistress; playing second string to wifey. You want to walk away but just how easy of a task is that to fulfill once that Love Jones comes down?"

~Linda R. Herman, author of *Consequences When Love Is Blind*

"Mistress Memoirs is a steamy fly-on-the-wall look over the shoulder of a sexy, successful woman who goes against her pristine upbringing and enters a world of taboo encounters. This book is a must have for those of us who wonder how can a woman sleep with a married man."

~Te'an Swington, Author of *SEXpressions*, the *Green Book*

"Mistress Memoirs is a spicy-hot, illicit liaison that readers will crave instantly. It's so good you can't help but want a second helping."

~OOSA Online Book Club

"In a fresh, new voice, debut novelist Lorraine Elzia "puts it out there" for married and committed women everywhere. In her "no-holds-barred" approach, she offers a privileged peek into the psyche of the universally despised mistress...interspersed with thought-provoking poetry."

~D.J. McLaurin, Author,
What If It Feels Good, and *Metamorphosis*

Affection and a need to belong are universal desires of man; the problem lies when one fulfills that need through the pursuit of Other People's Property.

~*Lorraine Elzia*

Prelude to an Affair

How did I get here? I am lost in a place where someone like me should never be. I am in the land of the other woman. The inhabitants of this domain, as my girlfriends and I perceive it, are uneducated "hood rats" with low self-esteem – playthings for married men. "*They*" are body parts, deliverers of mind blowing oral sex and equestrians in the art of riding. "*They*" have nothing to offer a man except their bodies. "*They*" aren't the type of women men are seen with in public places. Nor are "*They*" the type men take home to momma or big ma. "*They*" are those rump-shaking girls you see in rap videos – video whores adorned with weaves that reach the small of their backs. "*They*" are the kind of women that men hover over in dark, smoke-filled night clubs - scantily clad, moral-less creatures of the night, "*They*" are flesh, and lust, and appeal to the carnal hunger men possess and yearn for, and these same men pretend, in their perfect world not to know them if they see them on a Sunday afternoon in church.

I thought "*They*" were a lot of things, but I never thought "*They*" would be Me.

But here I am; his woman; his mistress; his night-time concubine and obsessed succubus. The potential home wrecker, the enabler, the whore, and I can't seem to pry myself loose from him. He has a hold on me now; mind, body and soul; and I can't let go. Occupying my veins, I am like a crack addict, totally addicted and always looking for the next time I can score. Hopefully, he'll find the Will and can let go for both of our sakes. For I have neither the Will nor the Strength.

Maybe it's a good idea to introduce myself. Although it really doesn't matter what my name is because I realize now I could be any woman, given the right set of circumstances. Every woman out there who says she would not mess around with a married man, needs to know that I said those very same words myself. It's conveniently easier said than done.

But for all practical purposes, I am Kahla, the total package. Well built, well raised, well educated, well groomed, well respected, well rounded, well-thy and any other adjective you can imagine beginning with well.

Clifton and Sandra Thompson accomplished their goal. They raised their only child, Kahla Marie Thompson, to be a pinnacle of success. I have done what most children strive to do to make their parents proud. I have shown them that all of their struggling to put me through high school and college paid off.

I am a Court Reporter for the Cook County District Court System, where notorious criminal felony cases in Chicago are tried. It's irony at its finest, when you think about it. I am a tool in facilitating the enforcement of morality during my nine to five, yet my actions barely register on the moral compass.

Standing at a succulent, five feet ten inches, and weighing in at a svelte one hundred and thirty-five pounds, I am beauty in its most pure form. Curves align my silhouette in every possible perfect way. My fierce walk, the bounce in my stride, deliberate and bold, coupled with the protrusion of a set of perky breasts and a round, sculpted behind has the ability to make men silently sing, *"She's a Brick House"* in their minds as I walk by. Without a doubt, I am the product of good genes. I thank my parents for that. Caramel-kissed, I am drenched with butter-soft skin and as my fine baby hair flows, dancing a jig around my face, I have what most people refer to as "good hair."

I own a home in Hyde Park off Lakeshore Drive; I eat at the finest restaurants Chicago has to offer, have a phat bank account, and drive a luxury car. I've got it going on, as they say, and I'm well aware of it. All of this was achieved through hard work, dedication and careful planning through the years to ensure that I stayed away from acquiring any unnecessary baggage, such as a husband or kids, along the way.

My parents taught me to reach my goals and never stray from the light at the end of the tunnel. They taught me that there would always be time "later" for the "baggage." They told me to make sure I made KAHLA all that KAHLA could be, so that I would never look back on my life and wonder what I COULD have been.

So I did it. I jumped through every hoop and hurdle and became a successful professional. I have no questions as to what I "might" have been in life, but now the question is, "Will I ever be wanted or loved?"

As Billy Dee said to Diana Ross in the movie *"Mahogany"*, "Success is nothing without someone to share it with." At the end of the day, when I've had the case from hell, and just want to come home to the arms of someone who can say, "Kahla, it's going to be all right," there is no one for that, no one to offer solace or comfort, no shoulder on which to lean or cry on.

So instead I drive my luxury car home to my big house on the hill, put on my silk pajamas, slipped into my satin sheets in my king size bed, and roll over, night after night to emptiness; and a bed that is continuously cold and lonely.

I do not have the luxury of being able to complain about the little things my married friends whine about: no one snoring; no one hogging the covers; or leaving toe nail clippings on the floor. There aren't any toys left at the front door for me to trip over; no dishes to wash; no laundry to do. I don't have to pick up other people's clothes left behind the bathroom door, and I don't have the option of complaining about what I have to cook for dinner, because I cook for only one person, and for me it is usually a *Lean Cuisine*. There is no one to fight with over the remote, or ask to turn down the music. There just isn't anyone to share anything with.

And that, my friends, is how he was able to get in. That feeling of loneliness, while lying in bed cold and alone night after night, is what opened the door and started my trip to the land of the other woman.

Appetizers and Entrée's

Contents

Geisha girl – a woman who is trained to provide entertaining and lighthearted company, especially for a man. One who captivates men.

Geisha Girl Kind of Mood

Tonight I'm in a Geisha Girl kind of mood.
Here for your enjoyment, fulfillment of your desires,
simply state to me what brings
your placid manhood to wood.
Tonight I'm in a subservient state of mind.
It's not my norm but…..I want to be a slave,
pleasing and performing for my master,
leaving all inhibitions behind.
Tell me what you secretly crave.
What makes your heart and member thump and grind,
because tonight, my paramour,
I'm in an obedient and freaky state of mind.
My limitations have been restricted;
the walls have been torn down.
State your wishes, your sexual indulgences,
upon them this voluntary harlot will not frown.
Corrupt my essence, debauch my thoughts,
capitalize on my Doppelganger presence and enjoy.
Seize and afflict my body and soul,
the window's open,
ignite passion and orgasms

17

to heights never attained before.

My alter ego has surfaced;

my resistance

and opposition have been confined.

Carpe Diem, (Seize the moment),

while I'm in this unusual and deviant,

Geisha Girl State of Mind.

Kahla

Eye Candy

There is an old saying, "don't sleep where you eat" and in retrospect, I realize that I have often used that saying as a defense mechanism to avoid relationships. It's been my own suit of armor and bullet proof vest of sorts, I never dated anyone where I worked, or anyone who I could potentially work with. This mantra of mine was born out of the realization that the chances of the relationship ending in disaster could burn a bridge I might later need to cross. And since in my mind, I could only date men of a certain respectable status, I alienated a large arena of men. I knew what I brought to the proverbial relationship table; looks, money, and a drama-free existence, so the barometer I used for male selection was very high. But I didn't worry about it at the time. I was young and there would always be time for a man and kids; or so I thought. But then it began, my biological clock was ticking so loud it was giving me a headache, and I began to let my guard down. I found myself sizing up ever man I saw. They all became pieces of sirloin meat to me, and *He* was no exception.

Lorraine Elzia

Kevin Eckhart was one of Chicago's finest; literally and figuratively speaking. He was an Illinois Police Officer. And like most women, I've always been a sucker for a man in uniform. Fire Fighters, Soldiers, Paramedics, and of course, anyone in law enforcement topped my list. Seeing Kevin that first time in his uniform, made me flash back to second Grade at Bushnell Elementary, when Mrs. Mable invited a local policeman to talk to our class about safety and how to protect ourselves from strangers. The officer told us to run away and scream at the top of our lungs for help if a stranger ever tried to abduct us. Scanning every inch of his uniform which was adorned with patches and ribbons, made me feel safe and secure; listening to his sultry baritone voice made me confident that whatever he said was the Gospel, plain and simple. At the end of his presentation to our class, the police officer seemed to effortlessly float down the narrow aisles of our classroom, passing tiny desk after tiny desk until he stopped at mine. I assume it was the star-struck look I had given him that made him come to me. He lifted me up out of my chair, carried me to the large, maple wood, teacher's desk and sat me on top of it. Then he took off his hat, put it on my head and said, "Sunshine, I hope you learned something today." I don't remember what I said in reply to his remark, but I do know that at the ripe old age of seven, I had acquired an insatiable hunger for policemen that I have never seemed to be able to shake.

My first encounter with Kevin was strictly in a professional capacity. We had taken a recess for lunch during a court hearing. As I walked out the courtroom doors and began passing each of the large, white marble pillars that were both a means of support for the building, and a means of intimidation for all who saw them, everything within my view seemed to be in slow motion and slightly out of focus, just like you see in those bad soft-porn movies. Even the consistent babble of the trial lawyer at my side seemed to muffle itself. The benches and old historic paintings of deceased justices that lined the walls of the courthouse all seemed to become a blur when *He* caught my eye. What a luscious and succulent piece of eye candy he was; and I enjoyed savoring the very sight of him.

Officer Kevin Eckhart was about six feet two inches, two hundred ten pounds, and his skin was a rich, dark-chocolate mixture that even on first sight, made my mouth water desiring to taste it. Kevin was "a tall drink of water on a hot day" as old folks used to say. His presence was the kind that dominates a room, thick and controlling like cigarette smoke, screaming to be acknowledged, instead of ignored. Kevin's aura was charismatic and alluring. Women and men alike couldn't help but be drawn to him when he entered within their vicinity. Even though there was hustling and bustling of people moving through the corridor of the courthouse, he still stood out. Among the sea of navy blue and other dark-colored conservative business suits, Kevin's Chicago Police Department issued uniform stood supreme. Those $2000 Armani suits had nothing on him.

His uniform fit him perfectly. It was "just tight enough" all over. The shirt was snug around the arms to reveal his "guns" as my girlfriends and I like to call them. And he had some massive guns, if I do say so myself – passionately deadly. His pants were "just tight enough" to let me see what he was working with, without being pornographic. And from what I could see, he definitely had the tools to keep a girl happy in that area. Eyeballing his spit-shined shoes, I noticed the size and secretly prayed I would have the chance to test the myth of shoe size versus penis size. He was holding his hat in his hand and slowly removing his mirrored sunglasses as I walked by. My radar was on and I began taking inventory of all of the ingredients used to make up Kevin. There was a fresh haircut, short and tapered around the ears with side burns that formed into a perfect letter V along his cheek line; almond brown, mesmerizing eyes, like two recently unwrapped Hershey kisses, and a perfectly trimmed mustache with matching goatee. One word described Kevin, and that word was "delicious." Another quick glance revealed there was no ring on the third finger of the left hand; no tan line either for that matter, so all was good. I don't know if married women hone in on that detail, but single women look at the ring finger almost instinctively. It's a detector of sorts that we possess. No ring is good, but you also have to check for tan lines to make sure the man didn't remove the ring just for the occasion.

Kevin smiled in my direction and that was the icing on the cake, the gravy on the taters, the crème de la crème. I couldn't see anything else but him as he turned and glanced my way; I melted. He had the whitest teeth I'd ever seen, sparkling like rays of sunshine, illuminating the air around him. Damn, I knew right then and there that I was a gone-ner. To me, there is nothing more sensual than a dark chocolate man with pearly white teeth; the Morris Chestnut type.

Butterflies and that warm, moist, tingly sensation invaded the center between my thighs. Yeah, it's sad to admit, but his mere appearance was enough to make me wet, he definitely was my type.

I instantly knew I was going to have to do my homework on him. Unquestionably, I'd have to let the *Girlfriend Network* check him out. After all, I had learned not to talk to every man who got my panties wet, or gave me that body-shaking tingly sensation. I'd had some scary mishaps in the past. Some of the men I found attractive had turned out to be less than desirable after checking with my *Girlfriend Network*. One guy had an active arrest warrant for family assault. He hit his girlfriend in the face with a beer bottle for giving him too much "lip service" during a super bowl game. Another one had some drug convictions or "mishaps during pharmaceutical sales" as he tried to explain it to me later. And yet another one had his car, his house, utilities and everything else he "owned" registered in his momma's name. Seeing as though I was not going to be anyone's sugar mama, I let that loser go as well.

Being a court reporter, I had made friends in practically every public service department. It helped my cases. Sometimes I need verification of spelling of names or addresses or industry terms. People speak a whole lot faster than most people realize, and it is often hard to decipher the names of some of the things they are testifying to. My *Girlfriend Network* could find out anything I wanted to know on someone, and was often more reliable than the CIA, FBI or even the best Private Investigator. All I had to do was call up the *Girlfriend Network* by nine a.m. and I would have a full, detailed life history of that person by my lunch hour. My girls did everything from running license plate numbers and credit reports to simple utility checks and Google.com. I would just give them a name, an approximate age, and watch them work their magic.

Since I could hear the "tick, tock" of my biological clock going off in my head, and Kevin looked like a perfect physical specimen to slow the clock down and lower the volume, I put out fillers for my girls to tell me what they could about him and I sat back waiting for all the information to pour in.

Ironically, it seems that as I was working my *Girlfriend Network*, so too, was Mr. Eckhart working the *Brotha Network*.

I received a call in my office mid-morning, the day after encountering my Eye-Candy. It wasn't from any of the members of my network; it was Greg, a long-time friend of mine. Our relationship was strictly platonic. I met him my freshman year in college at a fraternity party. We were both "DD", or *Designated Drivers* that night and while our friends were getting plastered and laid in the frat house, Greg and I played cards on the hood of his hooptie, waiting for the moment we were supposed to play taxi driver. Greg had a nice personality, but even from the first word out of his mouth, I knew he could never be anything more to me than a friend. He just did not have game like I was looking for, and his macking skills were like tarnished silver–desperately in need of polishing. He was not quite a nerd, just not "smooth" enough either. Greg married Tisha, his high-school sweetheart while we were still in college, and I had tapped the two of them on occasion to help try and find someone for me, but it never seemed to work out. When I began worrying about the ticking of my biological clock, I started networking my friends for potential mates. But all my friends were married, so their circle of friends was married, and so were their friends and so on, and so on.

Greg and I spoke frequently, so I thought nothing of his call that afternoon. After some idle chitchat, he cut to the chase.

"A partner of mine is digging you Kahla... he's sweating you bad."

"Oh, how so?" I responded nonchalantly.

"He's asking if you're married, dating anybody, have rug rats; that sort of thing."

Greg paused, as if to taunt me with his engaging and juicy bit of information. A coy smile emerged on my face because I realized that he knew me better than I thought.

I paused longer than expected, trying to play Greg's little game but my excitement coupled with anxiousness, dominated my stubbornness. So, I quickly rebutted, "Well, who is it? Anyone I'd be interested in?" My answer was coy, as I twirled the phone cord between my fingertips.

"I think he is your type, you know, *a refined thug*." Greg smirked and even though he was on the other end of the phone, I could vividly see his crooked grin and hear his muffled sarcasm.

I laughed inwardly, since all my friends knew I was looking for a doctor-gangsta or a lawyer-thug, a hooligan with a splash of class, a sophisticated ruffian making his paper. Someone with education, good looks, phat pockets, tight gear, and who liked to listen to the latest Macy Gray track while burning incense in a darkly lit room. They knew all I was looking for was the street look on a man of distinction.

"Well, Greg if he's my type, what's the delay? Why are you cock-blocking? Hook a sista up!"

"The more he asked about you, the quicker I put on the breaks. Kahla, it was Kevin Eckhart that was doing the inquiring."

I felt the bottom drop in my stomach and butterflies began to rise in its place. Mr. Eye Candy himself was interested in me? Umm, what an interesting thought. Images of Kevin and I naked, dripping with sweat and ram-shacking bedroom furniture as we made hot, monkey love instantly popped into my head like popcorn in a microwave.

"Good." I paused then continued, "I have been checking him out too. I think he is fine, without a doubt... somebody I would like to get to know, and I'm just waiting to see how he checks out with my friends. You know how I operate, Greg." I completed the statement with confidence as to mask my excitement and to play it cool. I wondered if Greg could see through my facade.

"Kahla, you know that man is married don't you?"

Silence. My heart began to race faster than a greyhound at a dog race. My lips were glued shut, my tongue refused to move.

I quickly ran my mental camcorder again. Nice face, tight body, beautiful smile, no ring tan line, and then I replied softly and less intense as before, "He didn't have on a ring when I saw him."

"He doesn't wear a ring Kahla, most cops don't. For one, they don't want perps to know they are married. People who commit crimes for a living will use anything they can against you. Knowledge of a wife can be a very useful emotional weapon because it adds vulnerability to a cop. Secondly, he's known as a playa, and playing is a lot easier without a ring. Some women don't care if a man is married, but some do. So a playa plays the odds and just doesn't wear a ring." Greg relayed this bit of knowledge, playa 101, on me as if it were common knowledge.

"Kahla, he's digging you, but I know him and you don't want to get involved. He's the love 'em and leave 'em type. He has more notches on his bed post than most people have clothes in their closet....or so I have been told. I told him I couldn't hook y'all up. That's just not my thing; hooking up married men with women they want to sleep with. If he were single, I'd be the host of *Blind Date* with you and him as my contestants. But helping a married man creep just isn't my style."

"Well, thanks for the info Greg. I have to go get ready for court."

I ended the call abruptly.

I was upset!

Lorraine Elzia

I must say I had slept well the night before, after seeing Kevin. He had brought upon a hardness that grew inside me that I was not able to shake for the rest of the day. The day before, when I left the courthouse I drove home and ran a hot luxurious bath with lots of bubbles. *Calgon, take me away.* Bubble baths always seemed to calm me, and the soothing, sedative fragrance of a hot, bath always had a way of lulling away the dust from my day.

Kevin had invaded every physical response of a stimulus within me and before I knew it, as I was taking my bath that day, the urges that normally only attacked me in my bed, began to overtake me right there in the bath tub, and I started fantasizing about him.

Soon my little man in the rowboat was being taken for a ride. As I massaged my lower lips, darting my fingers in and out, I imagined Kevin's fingers inside me instead of my own. Soon my juices were mixing with that of the Calgon and the hot water mixture already in the tub, as the ambience of the scented candles and sultry sounds of Saxophonist Najee encroached upon my senses and the bathroom. I arched my back in excitement and pinched my erect nipples hard, imagining it was Kevin doing the pinching and Kevin making me moan. I kept wringing my bath towel over my breast and as the hot water hit my nipples, I lightly blew air on them, knowing the breeze would cause them to get harder; a sensation I liked. I slithered around in the creamy stream I lay in and pressed my fingers deeper inside of me. A thrust of a finger followed by a pinching of a nipple until my breast began to hurt. It was the kind of "hurt so good" pain that makes your eyes roll to the back of your head. I kept repeating the cycle, thrust and pinch, thrust and pinch. I was playing with myself and thinking of Kevin. The feeling was thunderstorm electrifying, but I could only get to the boarder of ecstasy. I needed help crossing over. I squeezed my rowboat passenger harder and used the other hand to hit the button that turned on the Jacuzzi function of the tub. I moved my body so that the hard vibrating flow of the water could hit the right spot at just the right angle. It was just what I needed to take me over the top. I bit my bottom lip in rapturous delight, mostly in silence, except for a slight exhilarating moan, as my heart beat faster and faster then began to slow down. I kept my fingers deep inside me for a moment to keep both the pressure and the pleasure intact as the orgasm slowly began to subside--momentary beatitude to my desire. After my bath, I called it a night and drifted off with Kevin on my mind, a smile on my face and satisfaction between my legs.

That brief encounter at the courthouse with Kevin, made me horny and brought about a ray of hope that I would be beginning something new; A new relationship, a chance to be a part of a "we", and not just a "me" anymore. So my hopes had been high the night before my conversation with Greg, but after our conversation, everything was crushed.

"Why are all the good ones taken?" I asked myself in rhetorical fashion. "Who did I piss off? Or whose shit list did I get on that had caused me not to warrant just a little glimpse of romantic happiness?" I fervently rubbed my temples and moved my head side to side hearing the echoing cracking sound of released tension and bottled frustration.

I deserved someone good. I deserved to feel an orgasm brought about by the covetable hands of someone other than my own. "Why did he, and all the other good ones, have to be married?" That question hit me over the head like a ton of bricks. My eyes began to tighten, and I felt the salty taste of tears meet my angered, pouted lips.

The pity party had begun, and I had forgotten to bring a gift.

"Pull yourself together girl." My mind screamed in a megaphone of disgust at the cry for mercy I was begging for. "Oh well, this is just a slight set back," I tried to convince myself. "I'll get over it. I always do. I just have to keep looking. My Prince Charming was out there on his white horse, waiting to ride off into the glorious sunset; I just had to be patient and keep looking. When it was my time, God would send him to me. It just wasn't my time yet." I uttered those words defiantly, out loud to myself for encouragement. I knew I was too blessed by God to be stressing over a man, or lack thereof.

I did that sort of self-motivating talk often. Who needed Dr. Phil? I sure didn't, I had ME.

I learned early in adulthood that I had to uplift myself since there wasn't anyone else to do it for me. I tried to be supportive; I tried to be optimistic as I told myself half-heartedly, "I'd be okay. I could wait. I had waited that long, so I could wait longer." After all I wanted Mr. Right, not just Mr. Right Now.

And then I heard it again. The intensity of the sound was more obtrusive than before; almost as thunderous as a subway car barreling through an underground station. I could hear it get louder and louder... more nerve wrecking and piercing to my ears and thoughts than before...someone had turned up the volume on my biological clock until it was deafening to my ears... tick, tock, tick, tock, tick tock....

Crying of My Soul

My soul cried out in a language alien and

untranslatable to my ears.

A voice emerging from the murky abyss of my core,

yearning to be conjoined with the

accepted being of who I am.

It yelled to belong.

It cried to be heard.

To be listened to,

coddled, and assured.

It begged for permission to unwrap layers of false

confidence,

independence,

and esteem.

Offering to vacuum away the residue

of simulation and pretense,

leaving only carpet lines of an authentic being.

The volume intensified

and a part of me desired to give it recognition.

But true to the chameleon of my character,

I bond the voice and muffled the tears.

Lorraine Elzia

Pushing the mute button on my soul

until even I could not hear.

The weeping and wailing persisted,

yet my exterior shell of strength prevailed.

My soul continued to cry out,

But what landed were tears

that only silence held.

Kahla

Mr. Right

After Greg gave me the 411 on Kevin, I had pretty much put him out of my mind. After all, there was no way I was going to share a man, even if that man was really fine. Momma taught me better than that. So I went about my daily routine. I was a very busy person; I realize now in hindsight, that I involved myself in a lot of activities in order to fill up my time, to lessen the disappointing measurable periods spent at home alone. It's harder to be lonely when you have a multitude of activities on your plate to do. I knew the more time I had on my hands, the more likely I was to sit and have a "Pity Me" party. But if I kept myself busy, I didn't have much time to sit and envy my neighbors and friends--wishing I were in their shoes; wishing I could attend little league games and shop for SUV's.

So I kept myself busy, taking tennis, yoga and salsa dance lessons. I went to the gym five days a week for aerobics and weight training. I had a standing appointment every Friday to get my hair done, with a manicure and pedicure added in for special measure and then there was the shopping. I was a shop-a-holic. If there were a support group for people addicted to shopping I would have attend every meeting. I knew that I had a problem. It was an addiction for me. I spent more in one month on clothes than some households bring in. Every closet in my home was over-stocked with clothes, hats, shoes and purses. I literally could have worn a different outfit every day of the year with matching accessories and never repeated an outfit, if I wanted to. When all was said and done and I truly took the time to do some self-analysis, I realized that all the classes, self-pampering and especially the shopping helped to fill a void in my life. The void of not having a boo; a poppi; a sancho; a hubby or significant other. The clothes were my man, and the receipts were my children, and the more I collect of each, the smaller my void felt.

I really needed to get my knees ashy praying away my jealousy of married women. I needed to get a hold of the green-eyed crack pipe that had a hold of me. I knew I had to shake the monster that kept creeping up on me, and instead just enjoy my life as it was. That's what I told myself. I tried to listen…I tried to divert the negative energy.

Days after seeing Kevin that first time, I was out driving to the cleaners on my lunch hour, which was one of my usual errands. I typically went to a Korean cleaners and the lady that ran the shop loved to see me coming, we were on a first-name basis. To say I made her day each time I came through the door, would be an understatement. I had been keeping their store in business for a long time due to the amount of clothes I brought in for cleaning each month. As I was changing lanes, I heard sirens and saw red and blue lights flashing behind me; it was a police car. My heart began to beat a little faster as I tried to think what I had done wrong. I knew I had a lead foot, but that day I was just keeping up with traffic. *I haven't run any red lights or anything, so what could this be about?* I thought to myself as I looked in the rear-view mirror.

Mistress Memoirs

As I pulled to the side of the road and watched the officer approach my car, I reached over and got ready to hand him the things I knew he was going to ask for; Driver's License, Registration and Proof of Insurance. When the officer got to my window, I looked up and began to ask what I was being pulled over for, when I noticed I was looking in the face of Officer Eckhart.

"Well, hello caption lady, are you in some sort of rush?" He said brandishing those pearly whites.

It's not fair to fight with a loaded weapon, I thought to myself, but instead I said:

"Caption lady???? Do I know you?" *Smooth,* I thought; don't let him know you remember him. I reminded myself to pat myself on the back later for that one.

"And besides, I am pretty sure I was not speeding officer." I said with a coy smile.

"Oh, I guess I did not make as much of an impression on you as you did on me. I saw you at the courthouse. You're a Court Reporter right?"

"Yes, officer." I said. But why did you pull me over? I know I wasn't speeding."

"Well, Ms. Kahla Thompson, you know that, and I know that, but to keep this ticket from going downtown, you are going to have to be my guest for lunch."

I smiled. *Now he is really playing dirty,* I thought to myself as I stared at his massive arms. I was always a sucker for large biceps.

"I really don't think so, and how do you know my name?" I said, all the while smirking to myself at his smooth approach.

"Like I said, you made an impression on me, and I've got my sources. Awh... what's the problem? Even pretty girls like you gotta eat." He smirked, slowly removing his mirrored sunglasses so I could see the winking of his eye.

He was leaning over, practically inside my driver's-side window, and damn, he smelled so good. To the cars passing by on that warm summer day, everything looked on the up and up. A routine traffic stop, but Officer Eckhart and I both knew what time it was—Playtime.

"Come on girl; let me take you to lunch. There is nothing wrong with two professional people having lunch together. I'll follow you to any restaurant. You choose the place and I'll pay." He said, with those pearly whites smiling at me again. I envied the words that had the pleasure of slithering out of his mouth and over his lips. Damn he was sexy.

Money had never been an issue for me, but I never turned down a free meal either. Not to mention the fact that I hated eating alone and I was in straight-up flirt mode that day.

"Well, Officer, since I really don't want to get a ticket, I guess I will just have to go to lunch with you. Consider it my civic duty to obey officers of the law." I sarcastically commented, then batted my eyes like a southern bell. "Follow me." I took control.

I decided to play his game, to show him and myself that even though he could not have me, I still had skills to get him if I wanted to. I went to *Leona's*, an upscale restaurant near the lakefront; I chose it to get back at him for being attached and unavailable. I figured if all I could have from him was lunch I was going to make it worth my while. As I drove to the restaurant, I tried to justify my actions to myself. It worked.

"What are you doing and why are you doing this?" I asked myself. "There's nothing wrong with lunch. It's just two people eating. I go to lunch with guys all the time. So what if we are attracted to one another? It's just a lunch." I tried to rationalize. "Besides," I continued with my self-analyzing, "I really want the opportunity to bust him out about being married. I am going to tell him, "Yeah playa, playa" I know you're creeping, but I'm not the one to mess with."

Beads of hot sweat began to build up in the palms of my hands and my grip on the steering wheel was deathly tight. I practiced how I was going to lay out the fact that I knew he was married. I thought of several witty ways of saying it. My mind simmered with ideas to show him I had beaten him at his own game before losing my heart. I told myself that I was going to eat lunch, bust him out, and call it a day. "Perfect," I thought with a devilish grin.

But of course that is not what happened.

Officer Eckhart was ready for me also. He must have been anticipating my next move and prepared a game plan accordingly.

We arrived at *Leona's*, and as I pulled into a parking space, Kevin walked over before I could even turn off my car's ignition. He was there; first opening my car door, then the restaurant door, all the while guiding me in before him using his hand, placed in the small of my back.

It's funny how you remember little things like that about someone you love. I realized his gentlemanly gestures were so noticeable to me, and yet instinctive to him. I remember thinking, "Did his momma teach him that? Or was that part of the molding done by his wife?" "Interesting!" I pondered.

It's no secret that the existence of a woman in a man's life enhances him as a person. Most men are like a lump of clay and women mold them into an attractive work of art. A woman can change the way a man dresses, smells and acts. We teach a man what a woman likes and how she likes it, and then we wonder why they are taken from us by other women. The hands of a wife, mother or girlfriend teach a man the fine art of pleasing a woman. Whether his mannerisms were instilled in him by his mother or from his wife, I wanted them for myself.

Leona's was known for its atmosphere. Long burgundy velvet curtains, topped with textured sheer window scarves and tied with gold tassels adorned the windows. Large pieces of abstract art hung under elegant black-finished wall picture lights. Aztec wool-woven rugs lead the way to a cozy Bordeaux table for two and a dimly-lit Dale Tiffany piano lamp rested on the table. We were seated immediately. He pulled out my chair and sat directly across from me. I could smell the scent of *Acqua Di Gio by Giorgio Armani for Men*, which was my favorite. I wondered if it was a coincidence he was wearing it, or was his scent of the day a result of his background research of me and my tastes; but either way,

He got an 'A' for his ingenuity. I couldn't or should I say, "wouldn't" let on to him that I noticed he had it on.

Kevin removed his mirrored glasses and hat, slowly and temerarious were his movements. He had a suave and caviler quality about him. His hair was neatly trimmed and his side burns and goatee were immaculate, not a hair out of place. I shifted in my chair due to the warm feeling his appearance was creating between my thighs. I was having trouble maintaining eye contact because I did not want him to see that I was melting in his presence. Our waitress, a tall, slender woman with large olive shaped eyes, took our order and after she left, the small talk began.

"So madam captioner, how's business? Do you ever get tired of typing on that little machine of yours?"

"It's not typing, but no, I don't get tired of it. It's a reflex action for me. I've been doing it for so long that I can transcribe a trial word-for-word, without even paying attention to what is being said. I am usually balancing my checkbook in my head or thinking of errands I have to run."

"Multi-talented! I like that. So what do you do on your off time? I hear Denzel's new movie is opening this weekend," he said, in anticipation of a positive response from me.

I paused momentarily…just to create tension, and then I spoke, "What would your wife say about you taking me to the movies?" I responded, then grinned at my own mastery of the conversation.

He smirked at my remark. "I didn't ask you to go to the movies with me. I simply was telling you the movie started this weekend."

Damn! How did I slip into that? My coolness went right out the door. I felt embarrassed and like I had to clean up what I messed up very quickly to save face.

"Oh, just checking. Thanks for the entertainment update." I responded while rolling my eyes to give a nonchalant appearance.

"You're welcome. But if I had of asked you to go with me, would you have accepted?"

Wrong move handsome! I thought to myself. "If that is an invitation, I will go back to my original statement and ask you what your wife would think about you asking women to the movies?"

"Well, Caption Lady, since you have done quite a bit of homework for someone who didn't know who I was, I will set the scenario of how it is in the Eckhart home. Yes, I am married and have been for 10 years. I know this is going to sound like a line, but I will say it anyway. I am not happy at home and have not been for a very long time. The last four years to be exact."

"You're right Officer Eckhart. That does sound like a line." I leaned back in my chair and raised my eye brow judgmentally.

"Please call me Kevin." He commanded. Ooh…I loved the way the words rolled off his lips.

"Well, Kevin; like I was saying, it seems to me that if you are not happy at home you should leave instead of asking women out on dates."

"That's easier said than done, beautiful." Each syllable caressed me and he knew it.

Why did he have to go there? I was smiling despite my attempts to fight it. I am such a sucker for compliments and could feel my resistance to him lowering.

"Kahla…May I call you that?"

"Yes, you may. I prefer my given name, to you calling me Caption Lady."

"Since we have surpassed the small talk and gotten into the meat of our conversation, I will jump directly into it. I would like to get to know you better. In whatever capacity you will allow. I will tell you exactly what my situation is and let you be the judge and jury of who I am; fair enough?" His pleading eyes implored an answer. I regained control of the situation.

"Fair enough," I said, but in my mind I was thinking, "There is nothing you can say. I am not getting involved with a married man. Momma didn't raise no fool."

Kevin continued.

"I was in love at one time, or at least I thought I was. I realize now that it was not love, but that I got married more out of the need to do the right thing. My wife was pregnant at the time, and I was 20 something and thinking that it was time for me to settle down. You know, grow up, start a family, be responsible. So that is what I did. In the beginning things were good, but slowly I started to feel like we just weren't connecting. We are more like roommates. We share the household duties, the bills, the money, but not the love. She didn't know me and I didn't know her. We both had changed. It's like we out grew each other."

"So why not leave?" I replied. Divorce is not taboo these days, there's no shame in it. Why stay in something when you are not happy?" I anticipated him delivering tired lines about what was best for his child and that's exactly what he did.

"I made a vow to myself that I would never leave my family," he said. "I grew up without a father around and I suffered. I suffered mentally, physically and financially, and I will not let a child of mine go through that. Once you have kids, it is no longer about you. Your wants, your wishes and your dreams all become second to theirs."

"But Kevin, if you and your wife are not happy together don't you think your child feels that?" Kids are much smarter than we think they are."

"I think all my daughter can feel is that she is loved. She only knows that her home consist of mommy and daddy. We don't argue, fuss or fight. We are cordial and I don't think she senses anything as being wrong, because this is the way our home has always been for her-- it's all she knows."

"So, if you are not fighting, exactly what is wrong, and why are you telling me all this Kevin? Sounds like you need a marriage counselor. I am the wrong person to be telling this to since I am not married and never have been. I can't give advice on how to sustain marital bliss." I rolled my eyes with a sigh, to indicate my frustration at his situation.

"Look, Kahla. I know your friends have come back to you and told you that I am interested in you. I just want the chance to get to know you. You caught my eye a long time ago and it took me a while to build up the nerve to step to you. You are an intimidating woman; a brotha knows he has to come correct when he steps to you." He attempted a smile to steal one from me. It worked to say the least. Like I said, the man was smooth.

Seeing he was gaining ground, Kevin proceeded.

"A man looks at you and sees a very beautiful woman, but not just beauty, brains too--a woman with her head in the right place. She has everything going for her. She is unattached, no kids, no baggage, no drama. You have it all! A man says to himself, what can I give a woman like that, a woman who has everything? Especially when she achieved it all on her own. You are very intimidating Kahla, especially to a man who is married, and sees that all he can bring to your life, at this time, is drama." He looks down. His words dripped with honesty and pleaded for a rebuttal.

"And I'm not up for any drama," I said softly, recognizing he let his guard down.

"That's the reason I left you alone for so long." Kevin admitted. "But I like what I see in you, and I would like to get to know you. I would be a liar if I said that I wasn't interested in you sexually, but I am willing to just be your friend if that is all you will allow. Will you allow me to get to know you Kahla?" His eyes enhanced his petition.

"Will you let me have a piece of your world; no matter how small? I am not asking for your hand in marriage, hell, I got a wife. I'd just like to be your friend." I could hear raw conviction in his tone.

I sized up his proposal in my mind for a few minutes. He wore me down.

"Big Ma always told me you can never have too many friends, although I can tell you right now I am not getting involved with you or any other married man, I will accept your hand in friendship." I avoided eye contact and retained my insouciant vibe.

With that Kevin smiled, and now in hindsight, I swear it was more of a satanic grin, quite sinister in fact. Almost as if he knew he had me, right there at that moment, in that restaurant. Even then, I think he knew it was *"check and check mate."*

Welcome to Foreplay

Amicable days turned into convivial weeks, and Kevin and I began to bond. We told ourselves that we were *just friends*, but a relationship was slowly building. Our *friendship* seemed to barge its way passed the parameters that had once contained it. Kevin was very attentive to me. I didn't know if he was that way with his wife, or if he was like that with me because I was something new. Either way, he was pushing all the right buttons to control me. I thought I didn't want anything but his friendship, but what he was providing me I began to like and depend on immensely.

> *"Mi amor, yo no puedo esperar para hacer ambos conjunto*
> *de su sonrisa de labios."*

The sexy baritone sound of his invitation on my voice mail sent rhythmic vibrations from my ears to my thighs, causing me to squirm in my seat while listening. My mind performed two functions; first it translated the words for my enjoyment:

Lorraine Elzia

"My love, I can't wait to make both sets of your lips smile."

Second my mind tried to maintain awareness of my surroundings and the fact that I was driving and needed to keep my mind on the road and not on Kevin.

He left me voice messages like that every night on my cell phone so that I could hear his voice during rush-hour traffic in the morning. As I drove, I sent him a text message in reply:

"Set one of my lips is smiling and something tells me if I gave you half a chance, set two would be smiling as well."

Systematically, he followed his night call, which was usually filled with flirtatious sexual innuendos, with another call every morning once I got to work. The morning greeting usually began with, "Hello beautiful, how's my ray of sunshine today? I thought about you last night, which made for happy thoughts and wet dreams."

Butterflies were aflutter swarming in my stomach performing, *The Nutcracker*, or some other choreographed routine of their own as I thought that Kevin had to be a dream because reality could not be as invigorating.

Every time I heard his voice; I got that feeling you get on a rollercoaster on a downward plunge that just takes your breath away. – A shrill thrill.

I know it sounds corny, but when you are attention deprived like I was, you love that kind of stuff. When you're starved for attention, you don't care if the line is corny or cheesy, you just want to hear somebody say it; anybody say it; as long as they mean it. When you are starved for attention, you don't care what context he was thinking about you in, just as long as he was thinking about you. Period.

Relentless were his actions to keep my mind on him. I would receive at least three or four other calls from him throughout the day. Each time the phone rang; I'd look at the number on the caller ID and instantly got a smile on my face; in anticipation that his factitious banter would bring me joy. If he did not get me on the phone, he left messages on my answering machine. I realize now that he was masterfully covering his bases. He made sure he was the first thing I thought about in the morning when I woke up and the last thing I thought about at night when I went to bed. And it was working. The spider was definitely spinning a web for his fly. I must admit I loved it.

Kevin had a way of reading me; my every thought and desire and using the knowledge he gained to seduce me ever so slightly. He knew I was starved for attention, and he gave me the enthrallment I needed. His compliments were the hot air that the balloon of my mind needed to expand. His favorite line was:

"It has to be a sin to look as good as you do."

Or

"How do you resist touching yourself?"

Excellent foreplay, I thought. I was smitten.

Stimulating were the phone calls; spellbinding were the emails. He made sure he was in my blood by seducing my mind as well as my ears. Each day he would send me QOTDs (Questions of the Day) with his thoughts sprinkled in for me to marinate on.

Politics QOTD: Early voting has begun, have you exercised the right people died in order for you to have? I'm not telling you who to vote for, just trying to make sure you vote.

Religion QOTD: My favorite scripture is "Love Thy Neighbor." Have you shown love to your neighbor today? Do you consider me your neighbor? How about showing me some much needed love?"

With advanced knowledge reminiscent of that of a news reporter, he informed me of Celebrity Gossip;

Sports, and pressing World Events of the day; followed by a tantalizing note for good measure.

Hey Beautiful,

I was watching an interesting documentary on subliminal messages (Do Me Baby). The show said that sometimes (Do Me Baby) people put subliminal messages in the minds of others through regular conversation or even in emails. The show went on to say people do this so they can reach someone's subconscious thoughts (Do Me Baby, Do Me Baby, Do Me Baby). Can you believe someone would resort to such low tactics to make another person think about them? I'm so glad we met each other and that we are both (Do Me Baby) above tactics like that to try and persuade the other (Do Me Baby) to cross the line. Aren't you glad (Do Me Baby) we both are above that behavior?

Happy thoughts,

Kevin

The topics were endless; some comical, others were thought-provoking, marinating moments. But every word out of his mouth was tailored, I recognized as an afterthought, as foreplay and seduction. He played me like a violin and my mind gave in and played along in accompaniment to his erotic melody.

I wondered if he was the same way with his wife; or were all of his deeds just actions that faded over time.

Did he keep up the attentiveness?

Does any man?

And if he treated his wife in the same alluring manner, did she appreciate it as much as I did? Did she smile and feel childishly euphoric every time he complimented her, like I did? Or did she shrug him and his advances off with a sarcastic question like, "Okay, what do you want now?"

My mind was spinning with obsessive thoughts about how his wife could be letting such a succulent morsel of a man slip away from her.

"What is wrong with married women? Don't they know how good they have it? If I were married things would be different," or so I told myself.

My married friends would often say to me, "My husband is on me all the time; he acts like sex is a new toy and all he wants to do is play." My response was, "That's wonderful, if it weren't that way then there WOULD be a problem in your marriage. You're blessed to have a man that wants you so badly." The response I usually got to my opinionated statement was usually a rolling of the eyes, a frozen glance, followed by; "You just don't understand, Kahla."

Well, you know what? They were right. I didn't understand it at all.

Single girls want that kind of attention. The attention married girls complain about; we crave. And I, for one, knew if I got that kind of attention all the time, I would have loved it even more and been grateful to receive it.

I sat at the stop light with my eyes closed for a moment asking myself, "What are you doing? Has being single for so long caused you to resort to allowing this man to seduce you? That's what he's doing Kahla....It's seduction and you are allowing it." Slowly, I took a sip of my Mocha Chocolate Latte. Chocolate sooths the soul, I was hoping it would "shut up" voices as well.

Maybe that was the reason Kevin gave me so much attention. He could see the appreciation in my eyes, in my words, in my actions and reactions. I suppose he could see the way I blushed every time he gave me a compliment. I am sure he saw the giddiness and elation on my face. As much as I was starved for attention, I think Kevin was starved for the reaction he got from giving the attention. It makes a man feel like a real man when he can make a woman smile from his smoothness. It's a cause and effect situation, and we were becoming co-dependent on each other.

I found myself dressing differently; more provocatively. Taut were my dresses; accenting my curves. Shorter were my skirts; exposing the statuesque nature of my legs. One inch heels were replaced with two inch heels for added effect.

Did his wife still dress sexy for him? My mind began to wonder. Was she a frequent flyer of Victoria Secret like I was? Did she make sure that all of her underwear were silky soft with that "rip it off me" appeal?

Probably not. That's why he's creeping. She probably isn't taking care of home like she should; like I would. He deserves better. He deserves a woman like me. I'd make sure he never needed to stray if he were mine. I thought to myself.

Some of my married friends tend to dress kind of conservative; in housecoats, oversized baggy jeans and t-shirts or aged jogging suits. They dress up for special occasions, and of course in their Sunday finest for church, but not in the clothes that really turn a man on. Not the erotic, sexy stuff a man likes. Booty shorts, fish net body suits; satin bras and panties don't salaciously adorn their bodies; cotton is usually the underwear of choice for them.

Most married women just don't pay as much attention to the small details like a single woman does. They don't wear the form-fitting clothes that single women do, but often opt for a more comfortable look. My married friends have told me the reason for their wardrobe choice was that they didn't have the time to put into clothes that I did. They said that the time I put into myself, they had to put into getting kids dressed and ready for school or extra-curricular activities. That alone did not allow a lot of time for primping on themselves. Too bad for them; no sympathy from me.

My response? "Make the time. Remember that what you did to catch him, you should continue to do to keep him." But they should have known that already.

I told myself that my mindset would not change if I were married; but who knows? Maybe I would become less prissy if I had other people in my life to worry about other than myself. Maybe I would slip into that married woman rut. Maybe I would let myself go a little bit as well. I'm sure most married women thought the same thing when they were single; they probably thought they wouldn't change either. But over the years, slowly but surely, it happened. –The transformation from sex kitten to humdrum wife.

I am sure it was the comfort level that was the culprit allowing them to cease taking as much care of themselves. There is comfort in having a significant other, that's why single women want to be married. We are searching for that same level of stability.

When you have a man, what is the need in sprucing yourself up? What does it matter if you are carrying an extra tire around the middle? You already have a man, and you can always blame the fat you are carrying on the baby, on the fact that you have brought forth the fruit of his loins. Single women are always trying to catch a man, so we work harder at our appearance. Married women, especially those with a career and the household to run, aren't trying to catch anything except a few extra hours of sleep.

It's ironic that I was always trying to catch a man, and I dressed with that goal in mind, yet it seemed that all it took was a man showing a little bit of interest in me for me to pull out all the stops and bump it up to the next level.

Dressing nice was my practice, but on the off chance that I might see Kevin, I found myself wearing my more form-fitting suits to work. Even my conservative *Renee Dumarr* pants suits showed a little cleavage. And on the days I knew I wouldn't see him, I would still dress as professionally sexy as I could. I did this for two reasons: One, when I dressed sexier, I felt sexier, and I gave off more sexual vibes. I liked that self-confident aura that I was feeling within me.

And two, because I knew that one of the games Kevin liked to play was calling me on the phone and asking me, "What are you wearing today? Tell me in detail."

He would drop the tone of his voice each and every time he said it. Not quite Barry Whiteish, but low enough that it was a turn on for me. A tone that beckoned me to be bad. A tone that I could not resist. A tone that made love to my ears, and seduced my soul.

The loss of my phone-seduction virginity was lame that first time:

"I'm hungry KAHLA; feed me with thoughts of what you are wearing."

"Man you are crazy."

"Play along Sweetheart. FEED my mind with an appetizer of what I'm missing right now."

Okay, if it will get you off the subject. I have on a two piece crimson colored Kasper suit.

"More Kahla...give me more....What's underneath the jacket?"

"A silk camisole. – black." I answered almost annoyed.

"Does it peek through the top as you lean over? Whispering to all in your presence that your breasts want to be seen?"

"Laughing, I suppose it does Kevin." I was blushing. *"Can we move to another topic?"*

"Only if you tell me beautiful, what's under the camisole and say it slowly for me. Do that and we can move on."

I laughed again, then wickedly I answered..."NOTHING! Next Topic."

I loved the way he asked me to describe my clothing. And it wasn't so much that it was a request for the info, as much as it was an order for me to tell him. It made me feel so sexy giving into his desire verbally, if only just a little. Although I was not very good at seducing a man on the phone; after all, I had not done that sort of thing before, but as time went on and with coaxing from him, I found myself describing every article of clothing right down to my stockings, underwear, perfume and jewelry.

As I went about this daily ritual with Kevin, I got better at it. I noticed that I began to get into character for the call. I would tilt my head to one side, letting the length of my hair fall over my eyes as I closed them and rubbed my fingers through the softness of my hair to aid my mood as I described each article of clothing to him. The tone of my voice began to reek of sexiness. With practice, I soon sounded more like a phone-sex operator while performing this service for him. It was so comforting to me giving into him in that way. I got better at it over time and often took the lead.

This non-physical sexual event every morning turned me on more than some sexual encounters I had. I could hear his breathing change. It became labored as I told him what I was wearing. It slowed down; it deepened.

"I have on a two-piece red suit; clinging to my body like a second skin. Red pumps; shiny which scream with each step, 'Let me dominate you.' My hair is pinned up in the back with single ringlets hanging over my ears, exposing my neck, which longs to be kissed. A single gold necklace surrounds spots that your lips should be attached to, and I have on *Clive Christian* perfume; your favorite."

I could hear him relaxing and visualizing what I was telling him.

"Underneath my suit jacket, I have on a black, French cut, lace bra and panty set that snaps in the front for easy access."

He let out a verbal moan and I could hear him adjust himself in his seat as I continued.

Lorraine Elzia

"I couldn't find my regular panty hose, so I had to put on my black thigh-high stockings with garters."

He was shifting from one side to another and I knew this was due to excitement from my alluring words and the pitch in which I delivered them.

And even though the descriptions I gave did not get pornographic, we both would get turned on from the game we were playing. He got turned on by the picture I was painting, and I got turned on by him responding to my playful melody of words.

Sultry was the tone of his voice when he asked me to detail my clothing....that turned me on. The way he breathed as I described what I was wearing turned me on. The naughtiness of what he was asking me, and what we were doing turned me on. As much as I hated to admit it, everything about Kevin turned me on. His aura was like a hickie to my entire being...passionately placed in my mind. My body temperature rose, my nipples hardened and I could feel myself squeezing the muscles together between my thighs.

It had begun. The phone calls, the emails, and an occasional lunch were all an introduction to the illicit liaison that would follow. We were a playing with fire, as if we were unaware that we would eventually get burned; more than friends, but not quite lovers, at least not yet. And even though we had not gotten to physical intimacy, mental and emotional intimacy was definitely brewing.

I told myself, *"Welcome to Foreplay Kahla."* After all, that is what it was. We were enticing one another; stimulating one another, and most of all we were setting the stage of what was to come. We told ourselves that we were *just friends*, but we both knew we were deluding ourselves. Or at least, I knew I was deluding myself. I think Kevin knew from day one that he wanted more than a friendship. Men always want more than that. They want to be your lover, but will settle for being your friend. -It's all part of their head game; skillfully plotted for desired results.

I truly thought I could just be his *friend*. I truly thought that I could maintain control over my feelings, and keep them in check. I thought that my will power would be strong enough to keep everything in line, and I would just have a little innocent fun.

Lust, un-acted upon isn't a sin; right?

Or is it?

I realize now, that I thought wrong...terribly wrong.

The writing was on the wall and it was very clear that we were falling for each other, and falling hard. We said it was about *friendship*, but what we were doing was going through the motions of a booty call waiting to happen.

We enjoyed each other too much to just be *friends*. Maybe that was the problem. A man and a woman can be friends, as long as they do not *really* like each other. It is okay if they like each other, but if the *really* like each other than watch out!

They have to have a brother/sister relationship, not a relationship of good friends. If I could point to one thing that led this to be an affair instead of a friendship, I would say it was that we *really* liked each other. He was like one of the girls with bonuses. I gossiped with him, talked to him, joke with him and yet it had the added element of attraction. I *really* liked him. It was *too right* for us to just be *friends*.

I NEEDED him.

More so than I realized at the time. I got "that" feeling when he wasn't around.

I am sure at some point you have felt it, it's the feeling you get in the pit of your stomach, that gnawing feeling that makes it ache when you do not hear from the other person. You find yourself grumpy if you don't talk to them. You need that idle bull shit talk to get you through the day. I'm talking about the feeling where you don't want to eat or drink, or sleep. You don't want to go anywhere or do anything until you have heard their voice. That feeling that makes your mind drift when you are in the middle of conversations with others because you are thinking about them. A feeling of emptiness, a feeling of destitution, that's what it was like when he wasn't around. I did not want to go back to running on empty. He made me feel full and complete, and I liked that feeling much better.

"You are bright Kahla, why are you acting so stupid, why are you letting yourself fall for him? He's unobtainable, leave it alone." I heard that little voice in my head scream over and over again.

It kept telling me to stop the madness before it was too late. But my heart took over and I chose to follow its lead. I knew that I was falling for him, and I started telling myself I could love him from afar. I could be his *friend* on the outside; all the while secretly wanting him on the inside.

Things would still be okay.

He never had to know. I could control myself.

I was in control, not my heart.

I knew that I did not want to mess up his happy little home, so I would keep my feelings to myself. I could keep things in check; that was my rational. My head told me to run. Run like the wind…right then and there while I still had the chance. Remove him and all evidence of him from my life before it was too late. My mind knew I was slipping and falling, and it tried to warn me.

But I would not listen to my mind.

I knew that I wanted him to be part of my life and I fooled myself into thinking that I would be okay with what he was able to give. I told myself that what we were experiencing would suffice. *Friendship* would be enough.

Reality was that Kevin was a vice for me and just like every other vice in life; you can never get enough of it. And I could not get enough of him. Trying to enjoy Kevin in small dosages, with limitations, didn't work. He was like a morning cup of coffee that I had to have in order to start and sustain my day. Some people have a caffeine addiction, I had a Kevin compulsion. The cancer that was Kevin kept growing inside me, attaching it's roots and growing stems, even without the sex. I needed more, I wanted more, and before I realized it, Kevin and I had put ourselves on the path to have more. I was too stubborn to admit that I needed *affair* chemotherapy.

Unintentional Voyeur

Voyeuristic in nature,

I watched you today.

Soothed by your obliviousness to my existence

instead of dismayed.

The robe of daddy your wore

with attention and extreme care,

Pessimistically speaking,

the proper wear of this garment

is really rare.

Not merely a father,

the bearer of a seed,

But instead the precious term, "Daddy"

satisfying every need.

"Becoming", I mused,

as I watched you with your child.

Second nature to a real man,

begrudged by the buck wild.

My temperature raised;

Lorraine Elzia

nipples hardened,

excitement brewed,

as I was the recipient

of an unintended view into you.

An aphrodisiac of sorts;

analogous to Oedipus

with the sexes changed.

Rooted in adoration

in my own father's name.

Like a fly on the wall

I inhaled and I absorbed.

Relishing in the sight of

a black father on call.

I smiled as I fought the urge to speak

and I restrained myself at bay

Voyeuristic in nature,

I watched you today.

Kahla

Daddy Dearest

Bacteria filled, family pizza restaurants with oversized animatronics characters, arcade games, and snotty nosed kids running around screaming; have always been places I despised. But it was Jamal Quinton Murphy's sixth birthday, and he was my Godson, so I was obligated to appease Janae, my best friend, by not only attending the party, but being part of the wait staff to more than half a dozen sawed-off princes and pre-madonnas in his entourage.

I met Janae while in high school. She was chubby back then and taller than most of the guys in our class. With very little curves, she looked more like a linebacker for the Chicago Bears than a teenage girl. Half the seniors at Jefferson High School were afraid of her, including me. At seventeen, she already had a mouth full of gold teeth which made her whole persona much more menacing and predator like. But underneath her intimidating armor was a gentle giant with a heart of gold to match her mouth.

I got to know Janae's gentler side when my mother dropped me off at the skating rink for a party. I had just put on my skates and was standing around waiting for a familiar face to arrive when a group of boys came up to me from behind. One of them hit me on the butt, and then another boy did the same. I spun around to hit their hands, but all of them begin touching me at the same time. As I tried to fight off the boy's hands from groping me, I heard a voice say, "The next Neanderthal that puts his hands on her ass will draw back a nub." Even though Janae was a girl, she had punked the boys and they didn't want to see if she would make good on her promise so they left me alone. In one moment she had become my savior and my best friend and we were inseparable since that day. By the time we graduated from college, I had rubbed off on Janae and she had ditched her Tom Boy ways and transformed into a sassy woman with model like features.

As I looked across the table at Jamal, I smiled at his chiseled facial features and was happy with the fact that he had inherited his mom's "post" college looks. I picked up a Spiderman table cloth and began placing it on the table as I glanced around the restaurant. Everywhere within eye sight were tables sectioned off in the semi-large reception room, which reeked of the smell of Pepperoni and Parmesan Cheese. Themed decorations, balloons, streamers and signs indicating the names of all the boys and girls who were celebrating birthdays, covered the walls. Along with all the noise and germs floating around in the room, my eyes were bombarded with every cartoon character and superhero known to a child under the age of twelve. Suddenly there was a lull and the room got quiet as one of the groups began to sing:

Happy Birthday to you, Happy Birthday to you
Happy Birthday Dear Nicolette, Happy Birthday to
you.

Nicolette? I began to wonder where I had heard that name before. Then it dawned on me that I heard Kevin say it once. It was his daughter's name. Nicolette Cheyenne Eckhart. I remembered thinking when I heard him say her name, how beautiful it sounded as each syllable rolled across his tongue with fatherly pride.

Surveying the room in the direction of the singing, I caught a glimpse of Nicolette. She was sitting up on her knees in a small chair so that she could be higher as she blew out the candles on her *Cheetah Girl* cake. Her hair was innocently combed into two ponytails with leopard print ribbons around the top and the bottom portion hang loose down the small of her back. Nicolette had on a leopard skort set, the kind that looked like a skirt in the front but had shorts attached and along the bottom of her mini skort was a denim boarder. Very chic and it matched her party theme. Nicolette seemed to recognize the importance of coordinating the outfit with the occasion. As young as she was, her femininity was both apparent and impressive. She was dainty and prissy in her actions; a real girly girl. Her eyelashes were long and the almond shape of her dark brown eyes formed an angle at the corners, giving a kitten-like appearance to her face. As she puckered her lips to release air to blow out the candles, I saw that her front two teeth were missing. Instantly I knew Mr. and Mrs. Eckhart had probably taken advantage of a Sears photo special to memorialize that toothless grin. Every parent I knew had at least one toothless picture of their child on the fireplace mantle, and as pretty as Nicolette was, I knew her face was probably plastered all over the place in Kevin's living room.

I smiled at the precious sight before me with envy. And there, standing right behind her, as a daddy should be, was Kevin.

I heard a friend say once that "Coincidence is just God being Ambiguous."

Was it a coincidence that with all the pizza joints in Chicago, Kevin and I were in the same one?

I thought not.

I told myself I was supposed to see that side of him. He was my destiny; and that moment was meant to happen in order to solidify why I should "allow" him into my life. I rationalized that seeing him in a role other than seducer made it appropriate to "like" him as a friend. But in "affair after thought" I was probably being told to let the *Cosby's* be the *Cosby's* without my injection of "what if" into the equation. Kevin may not have been happy at home. But he

HAD a home – a family – a wife. If I weren't in the picture...if he didn't see possibilities of how life could be...maybe he would have been content.

Coincidence does not exist.

That moment was not happenstance.

God was being ambiguous and I misread His signs.– Subconsciously on purpose.

"Make sure you make a wish baby girl." Kevin smiled with pride as he looked in the direction of Nicole...his wife; the other part of the parental equation. I could almost hear the sound of tires coming to a screeching halt in my head as my mind stopped at a mental red light and shifted from watching Nicolette to acknowledging the existence of Nicole.

Starring at her like a deer caught in headlights, I couldn't take my eyes off of the accepted woman in Kevin's life.–His wife. I had often wondered what she looked like, but couldn't ever let on to him that I cared.

But I did care.

Every time Kevin left my presence I asked myself what SHE might be like, and why couldn't I be her.–The accepted one, instead of the woman on call; the dirty little secret on the downlow. I had envisioned Nicole as a homely woman, one that went unnoticed when she entered a room. Thinking of her as unattractive seemed to make being around him easier for me somehow. It was as if I were running a race against her and slowing winning the prize which was Kevin. She was my opponent, the only thing standing between me and the finish line of happily ever after.

Before seeing Nicole that day, I had often rehearsed a scene in my mind of our first encounter. In it, I thought that the first time I saw her, I would look at her eye to eye and say in my best *Shug Avery* interpretation from *The Color Purple*; "You sho' is ugly." But after seeing her, I realized those words wouldn't ever come from my lips concerning Mrs. Eckhart, because she was anything but ugly. In fact, we resembled each other. If I hadn't known better I would have sworn she was kin to me. The likeness was uncanny. Same age, same height, same figure, same hair, the only difference between us was the shade of our skin. I asked myself was Kevin pursuing me in an effort to just replace chocolate ice cream with butter pecan. It was clear what his taste was in women; and Nicole and I were cut from the same cookie mold, just one baked in her mother's womb a little longer than the other. Humans are creatures of habit. They like what they like. Kevin was no exception.

But our physical appearance was where the similarity ended.

As Kevin smiled in the direction of his wife, she seemed to return his smile with an impatient snarl. She seemed irritated that he was even looking in her direction.

"Are you going to take any pictures today Kevin? Or are you going to wait for the next time our daughter has a party before you capture the moment?" Nicole growled in rabid dog form over the singing. I raised my eyebrows to see if she was foaming at the mouth as well.

Kevin rolled his eyes, dismissing his wife's funky attitude and moved directly in front of Nicolette. "Smile for daddy honey."

"Cheese." Nicolette struck a pose with one hand on her hip with a large grin– minus two teeth. The girl was a natural ham.

"Can I open my gifts now Daddy? You said I could after we sang."

All of a sudden I felt a jab in my rib cage and I stopped watching the *Cosby Show* moment being reenacted in front of me. Janae was losing her patience with me.

"Did you come here to stare at kids all day or help me with Jamal's party? If I had known all you were going to do was stand around and try and look cute, I would have asked someone else to help me. Who are you staring at so intensely anyway? You act like God Almighty walked in here and you're about to be taken away in the Rapture."

Momentarily, I found amusement in the irony of her statement. The analogy was a perfect description of how I was beginning to feel about Kevin. The words were spoken by an outsider; but the feelings were mine. I owned them.

In my eyes Kevin was sent from up above and with each day I wanted to be taken away in the rapture of him. I wanted nothing more than to raise my hands in the air, open my legs and be taken to glory by him. I wanted to surrender my all and all to him. I saw a billboard at a church once that said, "Laying in bed screaming 'Oh God, Oh God!' won't get you into heaven. I swear each time I was around Kevin I wanted to test whether that was true or not.

"Hello!!! Are you listening to me Kahla?" I asked who are you staring at?" Janae said with less patience than before.

"I wasn't staring at anyone. I just happened to notice that Kevin's here." I looked down as I spoke, avoiding eye contact, placing napkins next to each of the plates hoping Janae wouldn't see through my charade and notice I was lying.

"Kevin who? I know you aren't talking about that shady ass police officer you had me check up on. Why do you care if he is here? I thought you left him alone once you found out he was married." Janae said as her judgmental eyes finally met mine.

"Girl, we are just friends." I lied again. "Besides, he plays a mean hand of spades and since you are so sorry at the game, I had to find someone to give me a little competition, to keep it interesting."

"SPADES!" Janae was practically screaming. "In what arena did you see his spades skills? Don't tell me he's been to your house Kahla."

I moved quickly to the other side of the table before I answered, just in case Janae forgot herself and thought I was her son and slapped me upside the head.

"Quit trippin' Nay'. He's only been over once or twice when he was on patrol in my neighborhood." Once again I avoided eye contact as I answered her.

"Kahla, you are the one who is trippin'. That man ain't ever been assigned to your neighborhood for patrol. That's just his story, he's sticking to it, and you are a fool for believing it. Yeah…he's patrolling alright. He's patrolling YOU like a dog pissing on its territory." Janae raised her leg imitating a dog urinating and made a sucking sound with her tongue against her teeth as she waited for my reply.

"Where are the tokens ma? We want to play some games before cutting the cake."

Jamal's question saved me from having to continue the conversation.

"I'll pass out the tokens Janae; you continue to set everything up. I'll be back." I winked at her in recognition that I knew my ass had just been saved from a chewing out, and I began to follow Jamal, happy to have escaped a beating.

Jamal's party entourage was lined up with their hands stretched out eagerly awaiting the tokens. I walked down the line giving each of them the ammo they desperately craved and watched them run off one by one in all directions with pubescent glee.

"Faster daddy. Go Faster."

I heard Nicolette as if she were the only one in the room.

I maneuvered myself behind a large arcade game and pretended to play it as I watched Kevin with Nicolette. She sat in his lap in a simulated Andretti Racing game.

The entire machine shook and slid side to side, jolting father and daughter in the process. The look of shock and amazement engulfed both of them. Kevin allowed Nicolette to steer as he pushed the pedals and shifted the gears. He let her run the controls and he continually gave her praise at each successful evasive move she made. Nicolette was ecstatic and Kevin was encouraging. After that game they played several others; all with the same outcome; daddy and his little girl bonding. In between games Nicolette would grab Kevin's hands and pull him to the next machine she wanted to play. I watched as Kevin pampered, gratified and satisfied every self-indulgent need of his daughter.

Watching him with her made me smile.

I wanted to be his wife; watching him with OUR daughter.

I wanted THAT life.

I walked back to the area where Janae was, and as if in a daze, I went through the superficial motions of helping Jamal open gifts as I observed Janae smile with satisfaction at the happiness experienced by her son.

Parental love was ramped in the building.

A feeling of loneliness filled me.

In panoramic vision, I scanned the room, and the scene was the same everywhere I looked; families smiling; parents recording precious moments in their minds. Laughter. Happiness.

Instinctively, I rubbed my stomach and sighed at the fact that it was empty and had never brought forth fruit.

Instantly, I felt like a failure. My life meant nothing as I viewed the sights before me. Right then the degrees, the house, the job, all of the material stuff meant nothing to me. I wanted nothing more than to trade it all in to be on the other side of the white picket fence, so to speak.

To me, the grass looked greener on the other side. More plush, more comfortable, and I wanted to trade in what I had in exchange for a piece of what I was witnessing all around me, and especially what I witnessed with Kevin and his daughter. I wanted to run my feet in the grass of family life. Not just momentarily, but forever.

I couldn't take it any longer. I made an excuse to Janae of having a transcript to complete before the morning. As I made my way to the door to leave, I saw Nicole. She was bellowing instructions to Kevin to hurry up and pack up their child's presents and take them to the car. He humbly obliged.

He never noticed me that day.

There was no pretense in his actions designed for my benefit.

He was just being himself; unaware of the fact that he was being watched.

Before being a spectator of Daddy Dearest, I thought I was falling in love with Kevin. After observing him in that role, I knew I was.

Sulking, I walked to my car. Nicole was a passenger in my mind. I tried to unbuckle her seat belt and make her get out my head, but I could not remove her no matter how hard I tried.

Mistress Memoirs

I began to weigh why Kevin should be with me instead of her; praying that as he went through the process of judging the two contestants vying for him, maybe, just maybe...he would see the obvious.

Where she was neglectful; I was attentive.

Where she was abusive; I was loving.

Where she was humdrum and boring; I was exciting.

Where she was weak; I was strong.

The scales should have been over abundantly tilted in my favor. Well, at least in my mind they were. And when it comes to winning the game, it only matters what exists in the winner's mind.

Somber was my mood as I open the car door and sat in the front seat. As I put my hand on the steering wheel, my imagination took flight and focused on the ring finger of my left hand. That finger was ring less; the same was true of Kevin's. In my case there was no ring because I had not yet taken a leap of matrimonial faith. In Kevin's case it was stated by Greg that Kevin didn't wear it because of his job. Well, maybe just maybe he didn't wear it for another reason.

A wedding ring, small and inconsequential is a symbol; the symbol of a complete circle of love. I told myself – subconsciously on purpose yet again, that he didn't wear a ring because his circle was not complete. The role of daddy took the lines of his marriage half way; but there was no love to round it out.

A self-serving theory, I admit that.

But one I chose to believe.

Nicole didn't value her husband, but I did. I gave myself plausible reasoning for my desires and the need to act on them.

Previously I had cared about being a part of separating a family, but that care was quickly leaving my thoughts.

Why should Kevin and I *both* suffer because Nicole had not had "her" man appraised and did not recognize his worth?

As I turned the ignition in the car, I reconciled the fact that one woman's trash is another woman's treasure.

And in that instance, all of a sudden garbage collecting seemed like a much more honorable job to me.

Break Glass in Case of Emergency

Kevin and I were progressing beyond the small stuff, our friendship barged its way passed the parameters that used to contain it. Lunches became dinners out, and dinners out soon became dinners in. "In" being at my house. Now in the scheme of friendships, anything done during the day is acceptable, but things done under the cloak of night become a gray area and Kevin and I were riding the tidal wave of gray.

Being a police officer, Kevin worked strange hours so it was easy for him to explain away his not being home in the evening to his wife. He would tell her his shift had been changed, someone called in and he had to cover, or that they were working a sting operation, that sort of thing. She always bought into his excuses, or at least she acted like she did because she could care less about his whereabouts.

The first couple of times we went to dinner, we were careful; we were very much aware of what the perception of others would be if we were seen together in public by people either of us knew. Even if we knew we weren't having sex, the perception by those seeing us would be that we were; an extended guilt by association scenario.

So we went to small, cozy restaurants in remote places on the outskirts of town. Our discussions consisted of how much we enjoyed each other's company and wanted to see each other, but that we didn't want to break up his happy home, or sully my reputation due to our wants or our desires. Not to mention the effect a scandal would have on his career. Police officers are supposed to be of high moral character. So we decided we would keep that aspect *in check*. We kept it discreet. We were at a point of seeing each other almost every day, so we soon decided that we could not be seen in public, it was too risky for both of us. The only natural solution was to start having dinners at my house.

Seeing each other at my house made it easier for Kevin to become my "Emergency dick in a glass" as I had heard a comedian once say. I think that is the role most male friends play in a woman's life. The men are there for us. Emotionally they provide support, someone to laugh with and a shoulder to cry on. Male friends can be that warm hug from big strong arms that a woman needs to feel every now and then. Male friends are mental outlets. You can talk to them about what you feel or think without the *cattiness* that sometimes comes with talking to other women.

Male friends are there emotionally and mentally. They just cannot cross the boundary into the physical. When a man is put in *friendship mode* with a woman, he stays "in his place' in order to be near her and be part of her life. He understands that part of her attraction to him is that he is a MAN, but he is not trying to "get some." That makes the woman trust him and makes her find him more appealing. The man knows this, so he does not cross over the line into the physical. He just sits back and patiently waits; hoping and wishing that one day the physical aspect will be added to the relationship.

All male friends do this whether consciously or subconsciously. In the back of his mind he hopes that one day she will want him "in that way." He hopes that all the groundwork he has been laying will pay off, and she will eventually see that he is really what she has been searching for. He is patient, hanging around like the fire extinguisher on the kitchen wall; always there when you need it.

He is there in case of an emergency; all she would have to do is break the glass. Should she need a sexual outlet and have no other avenue. He would be there. If the pipes need a little cleaning, even though he is "just a friend", he would be there. He waits for an opportunity, any opening, a chance to get his foot in the door. He knows that eventually the time will come where he will be needed and used.

Having dinner at my house did raise the comfort level between Kevin and me. There is something about a home cooked meal in a cozy environment that stimulates intimacy. We started off having dinner in my formal dining room at opposite ends of a grand table. That lasted for only a short time. Mostly we ate in my living room in front of the fireplace sitting on the floor. It became an automatic reflex for me to set a stage for our dinners. The ambience was one of romance that consisted of me lighting candles or dimming the lights. Sometimes we'd light a fire and pop in a Jazz CD or India Arie. After dinner we would sit next to each other on the floor, play a board game, Spades, watch TV, or just hang out. Being with him was like being with one of the girls–only different. We were almost too comfortable around one another. But that was okay because we were *just friends*; right?

Yeah right!

On one of those occasions as I was making dinner, Kevin came up behind me in the kitchen with no warning and slide his arms around my waist. I jumped a little since I was startled by his action. But the warmth of him against me was welcomed and sent chills down my spine. I had pinned my hair up when I came home and he began kissing the nape of my exposed neck. Instantly, I could feel the hairs on my neck begin to stand up on ends and I got butterflies in the pit of my stomach. I must admit I had envisioned that the moment would happen, even hoped and probably secretly prayed that it would. But I had been pushing those thoughts aside telling myself that we were, after all *"just friends."*

"What are you doing Kevin?" I tried with little force to get away, but he held me firmly in place. As if he knew I was saying *no*, but just needed coaxing to say *yes*.

"What does it look and feel like Kahla? I hope it hasn't been that long since you've been touched that you don't recognize it."

He continued kissing my neck and nibbling on my ear lobes. The room seemed to get hotter and I began to feel light headed. His lips were soft and comforting to my neck, like they belonged there, like they were at home.

"Tell me to stop," he whispered seductively in my ear, "and I will. Tell me you don't want me, and I'll leave. Just say the word, and I will do as you say. I won't pressure you to do anything you don't want to. But I know you won't say it Kahla. I think you want me just as much as I want you."

"We said we weren't going to do this," was my weak reply.

Why didn't I say "stop"?

Why didn't I just say THAT word?

With that he turned me around and before I knew it, he was kissing me. Long, deep and hard. Thick, warm and inviting was his tongue as it darted in and out of my mouth. He paused only long enough to suck on my bottom lip every now and then. I resisted at first, weakly, but I did resist. I was pushing against him, but he held me firmly against his chest, just the way I liked to be held. The scent of his body made me hungry for more and I soon felt my resistance weaning. I was giving in.

"Say STOP and I will." Kevin whispered.

I heard his words in my head and thought I could say it, but I couldn't. I swear the kiss being shared at that moment was the best kiss I had ever had; so passionate, so erotic, and so right.

But was it really?

Or did it seem that way simply because I had not kissed anyone in such a long time?

Or was it because it was him and I NEEDED him so badly?

His hands began to roam, rubbing my back and then fumbling with the knot of my white linen wrap around shirt that was tied in the front at my waist. His capable hands soon figured out the puzzle and were able to undo the maze.

I watched the whole scene as a spectator.

There goes my shirt dropping to the floor, there goes my bra dropping to the floor, and finally there goes my resistance dropping to the floor along with everything else.

Half naked in my kitchen, I heard the words of my head: "Stop him. What are you doing?"

But my body became jelly and wouldn't listen. Although from the inside, my head screamed the words; from the outside, my lips were on strike and refused to vocalize them so that they could be heard.

I could feel stiffness in my exposed nipples and I knew what was coming next. As he pressed me against the kitchen counter he began kissing down my body. His lips felt so good on my neck and as he made his way southward and began to suck my nipples I was covered in chill bumps. My heart was racing, my temperature was rising and I was excited to a point where I was sure he could see steam coming from my body.

I tried to snap out of it, tried to bring myself back to reality.

I began to have visions of his happy home running through my mind, thoughts of his wife in their kitchen cooking for him and his child. Then came thoughts of Nicolette playing in the backyard; swinging on the wooden play set Kevin had built for her.

Finally came the thoughts of me ruining that happy home.

Me causing his wife to scream and throw things.

Me causing his daughter to cry.

Me bursting that bubble of serene family life.

"Stop him, Kahla," my head echoed the thought. My mind was spinning with confusion.

My body tuned the thought out and began to sway with him, grinding into him, back and forth, harder and harder as he reached down and began rubbing between my thighs as he sucked on my neck. My back began to arch and I could feel his manhood rise as he pressed against me--instantly I was wet.

I allowed it.

I allowed myself to let go and enjoy it. My mind was wandering in sexual anticipation.

I wanted him so bad.

"I can't be the other woman, I won't." I said to myself.

Or would I?

Could I?

What he was doing to me felt so good and so right, even if only for right then. I did not want it to stop.

"Stop him Kahla, listen to me." My head was screaming for my compliance.

"NO!" Was the answer from my heart and my body.

With that answer; that approval to proceed, I slowly moved away from caring about his happy home and his family. I realized I was in a "damned if I do, damned if I don't situation." Either his family would suffer if I did give into my desires; or I would suffer if I didn't, because I was mentally and physically aching for him. Either way, someone was damned.

"Stop him Kahla, just say the word." My head continued to plead its case.

And then I felt my lips move.

"Finally," I thought, "at last I would stop the madness. I was attempting to form a word."

That's when I heard a voice--my voice, and it said, **"YES!"**

"Yes Kevin. Yes." Passion emitted with each word. I felt my body go limp as if every muscle in my body had relaxed and every part of my being had consented to surrender.

Prissy, uptight, morally righteous Kahla was gone, and my inner being that was self-centered remained.

I no longer cared about what I was ruining. I only cared about having my pipes cleaned; even if that meant I had to share.

I knew what I SHOULD have said, what would have been the right course of action to take, but instead, I started telling myself that I COULD share and that I WOULD share.

Hey, they teach you that in kindergarten; right?

Share and share alike. Play nicely and share your toys.

So why not? At least for sexual purposes, why not share?

As we moaned and groaned and grinded with each other, I decided he could stay home with "wifey" and still break me off a little somethin' somethin' every now and then. As a matter of fact it had been a long time since my pipes had been cleaned and I needed it bad.

And I wanted it from him. I decided, right then and there in the middle of my kitchen, half dressed with my breasts in Kevin's mouth, that I COULD share this man with his wife. I loved what he was doing and I didn't want it to stop.

All of a sudden, I COULDN'T hear my head say, "Stop him Kahla" anymore.

All I could hear was the sound of breaking glass and I realized that I had just shattered my "EMERGENCY DICK IN A GLASS KIT."

Platonic

With all that we have shared.
Can we ever be platonic?

As deeply as we have loved,
as deeply as we have cared
Can we ever be platonic?

Casual meeting....
staying within
the matrimonial lines
feelings of love......
mutual stimulation
we both try to hide

Can we ever be platonic?

Vows to another
you made long ago
intense sexual stimulation
we both try now not to show

Can we ever be platonic?

The answer is a resounding NO!!!
It's not possible......
Let's be realistic.....
The realm of being PLATONIC
we have to Let go.

There's too much love,
too much caring

Lorraine Elzia

love awakened
heart strings caressed within there
begin to show

We could never be PLATONIC

The word is
"SINFUL"
at least when it relates to us.
We would never be PLATONIC
for we are driven by lust.

We can't be friends
when lovers is what we desire.
We can't talk of our current
achievements
or social status
when sexual tension
ignites our fire.

Our tongues get tied
when trying to conversate
We are both aware
that our thoughts,
wishes and intentions,
simply want to copulate.

We fought temptation,
and chose to honor stated vows.
Avoid each other we must.......
especially since our lust has been aroused.

Mistress Memoirs

Love you as I do,
and love you
as I always will
"Platonic friends"
is a title our souls
and our hearts
could never fulfill

Sweet prince,
we can never
be less than lovers,
mere friends is not our choice to pick

We have to face it.....
my lover,
we could never be PLATONIC.

Kahla

Affair Consummation

Hearing me say "yes" was the green light Kevin had been waiting for. As if on cue and moving instinctively, he stopped what he was doing and lowered himself to one knee. His abrupt action left me standing before him panting heavily wanting more.

Running my fingers through my disheveled hair I said, "Why are you stopping now? You have to finish what you started." The words from my lips were almost unintelligible.

"Shh!" He replied with a crescent smile as he cupped his hands around my ankles and slowly yet methodically ran his hands up my claves.

"Oh so soft." He muttered.

Then up my thighs, messaging and caressing upwards still.

"Like a baby's cheek begging to be kissed." He proclaimed.

My legs began to tremble uncontrollably under his touch. I braced myself against the kitchen counter just in case I fell.

He began to gently spread my legs apart and he looked me directly in the eyes as he did so. Seductively he licked his lips, biting the bottom one in anticipation, I began to wonder if he had taken a course in how to make a woman wet via lip licking alone. He smiled as he inserted his finger inside me again. I gazed back at him with eager anticipation as I welcomed the feeling.

One insertion, passionately delivered was all I received this time.

"You're such a tease." I enticingly whispered.

He removed his finger, placed it in his mouth, and sucked it generously as if it were water to a man dying of thirst.

"Just like honey to a bear," he murmured as he ran his tongue from corner to corner of his mouth ensuring he had not missed a single drop of my juices.

Gradually Kevin began to rise from his knees, running his hands along my body in the process. He began removing the rest of my clothing and I aided his movements. Once I was completely naked, I felt an instinctive urge to place my hands over my breast to cover myself, but he removed my human shield as quickly as I had placed it there.

"Michael Angelo couldn't have created a better work of art. You are magnificent; a beauty only God could make."

I blushed at his comments, and thanked God Kevin had been born.

"I want this to be right Kahla. I want us both to remember this moment until we die." He was preaching to the choir, because I already knew it was a moment I would never forget.

Kevin whisked me off my feet with one strong hand and caressed my face with the other. We kissed again as he carried me through the threshold of the living room and ascended the spiral staircase towards my bedroom. He spoke no words, just stared into my eyes as he carried me to our destination.

"I guess talking isn't on the menu tonight," I whispered in staggered words, since he had taken my breath away when picking me up.

"No, but you are. We've done enough talking for a lifetime, tonight is about actions not about words."

We had intrigued each other with sexual promises and innuendo, but Kevin made it clear to me that it was time to make deposits on all the promises made.

He stopped at the door to my bedroom and smiled a salacious grin right before his pearly whites separated and his mouth began to ravish mine. His breath was minty fresh, I wondered if he has slipped an Altoid in his mouth after tasting his fingers in my kitchen, and I hoped my breath tasted as good to him as his did to me. I was pleased with his looks, his smell, his aura and I allowed my mouth to continue to melt in his. His kiss was urgent, more than just simple want. It was a 911 call of a man in need. He slowly and gently laid me on the bed and looked a little distracted for a moment. He was surveying my bedroom; looking for something. As if a light bulb went off, he walked over to the dresser and removed a red silk scarf that I used for wrapping my hair at night.

"Sit up." It was a deliberate request from his lips.

I obliged.

He placed the scarf over my eyes, tied it in back of my head and then gently raised my arms over my head interlocking my fingertips with his own. He ran his nose along the side of my face as if he were inhaling all of me. He began to kiss me again, this time squeezing our hands together in the same rhythm danced to by our lips. Still under the darkness of the scarf, my heart beat faster from his cloak of intrigue. I liked games and found him to be a worthy opponent.

"Don't move. Just lie back, and let me please you," were the next words my lover whispered as he nibbled on my ear and nuzzled his nose along the nape of my neck. His mouth lingered around my ears long enough to let the heat of his breath seduce my senses. I could feel my body temperature rise and I allowed myself to enjoy the heat of his breath and the heat of the moment.

Kevin moved his mouth directly in front of mine. I couldn't see his face from under the scarf, but felt him sucking my lips.

"Do you want me?" He asked the question as he ran his fingers across my lips.

"Is that a rhetorical question?" I coyly answered as I sucked his fingertips.

"Sometimes we have to wait patiently for the things we want." Kevin said the words as he rose up off of me, and I could tell he was leaving the room.

"What are you doing, where are you going?" I asked as I began to sit up.

"Don't move sunshine. Lie back down and be patient. Good things come to those that wait."

I relaxed on the bed and did as I was told. He had an ability to give me orders and yet make me feel delighted in being subservient to his commands. He was only gone for a brief moment or two and I could hear him as he came back into the room.

It was dark under the scarf and I couldn't see a thing, but I knew he was staring at my exposed body. Studying me.

I gyrated slowly on the bed seductively adding to the show.

I heard the sound of him unbuckling his belt and removing his pants, followed by more sounds of clothing hitting the floor. I tried to remain obedient, but it was hard not to move. I waited patiently as I had been instructed to do.

Kevin began crawling up my body, rubbing his nakedness against mine. Caressing and kissing each part of me as he ventured his way upward. The warmth of both his breath and his passion made me excited that I had decided to say "yes" to the moment.

I breathed a sigh of relief and said to myself, "I have no regrets."

He allowed his fingertips to lead, followed by his tongue on a mapped out course of passionate consumption of my skin. His touch was soft, yet hungry; all the while he was slowly licking every single inch of me. Each seductive caress and devouring lick gave way to moans from my lips and grinding of my hips underneath him. He was slow and methodical, relishing the movements of my body.

Mistress Memoirs

Kevin paused for a moment, and I could hear him reaching for something on the night stand. I couldn't see what it was, but it sounded like something clicking against glass.

Soon I was aware of what his little mission outside of the room was for. He reached into a glass that he had brought up from downstairs and placed on the night stand. There was no liquid in it; only ice. Kevin removed an ice cube and placed it in his mouth.

I let out a moan of anticipation as I felt him hover over my body. I sighed with pleasure as he erotically used his mouth to hold the ice as he outlined the silhouette of my breasts, leaving raised chill bumps and cold beads of moisture on my nipples. Uncontrollably I arched my back as he made a trail of ice water from my nipples down the center of my body and began to lower his head between my thighs.

My eyes rolled back in my head underneath the silk scarf; that moment was like losing my virginity all over again. I smiled and thought about the Spanish message he had left a few days earlier and said to myself, *"Set one of my lips always smiled around Kevin, but NOW set two was smiling as well."*

Everything He said He would Be

I'm basking in the afterglow
With sore thighs and a satisfied libido

He was everything he said he would be

Kissing me ever so gingerly
Slowly
Passionately
No inch of my skin left
Unkissed...
Untouched

Taking his time
Forcing me
To let go and enjoy him
PLEASING ME

He was everything he said he would be

He had paid attention to my previous cries of desire
Evident in his subtleties

As I came and came
I fought the urge to scream his name.

Punnani Connoisseur was he
Reaching spots never roamed
creating a sensual memory

And through it all giving to me,
the most erotic gestures of all
He talked
He listened
He shared some of himself with me

Lorraine Elzia

Exhaling with contentment while I reminiscence
He was everything he said he would be

Kahla

Bitter Sweet Pillow Talk

That first sexual encounter with Kevin was bitter sweet. Afterwards, while basking in the after glow of continuous orgasms, I had all the feelings you would expect. The bitter was one of remorse, sadness and shame.

I was remorseful thinking "How could I do that to another woman; to his wife? Didn't I owe her something? Shouldn't there have been a sisterhood among women? Aren't we supposed to look out for one another just by virtue of our shared sex? Why was I allowing myself to be a tool in destroying their marriage?"

I felt sadness. Sad that he couldn't be mine, and if he were ever mine, would I ever be able to trust him? He had cheated on her with me, so why wouldn't he do it again with me playing the victim's role? I was sad that I had experienced passion and love, but could not have it for my very own, at least not with him. And of course, I had extreme shame at myself for sinking to a point where I would take half a man over no man at all. I had an overwhelming shame that someone like me, someone with everything going for herself had fallen for "game" and had become the other woman.

The sweetness was the experience itself. The kissing and the sex were so passionate. When our lips met it was electrifying. An experience I could spend the rest of my waking days and nights indulging in. I had laid in his arms as Kevin ran his fingers through my hair. A purr emitted from my soul and I closed my eyes as the pillow talk began.

I lay across his body with my head resting on his chest. I ran my fingernails up and down his rock hard chest admiring how firm and hard his pectoral muscles were.

Is that the result of numerous hours in a gym or a kiss to his genes from God, I mused.

He was so manly; so virile. I nuzzled my nose closer to his chest and inhaled the musk scent of his skin that was ambrosia to my nostrils.

While allowing my hands to canvas ever inch of his smooth chocolate skin, I noticed a raised scar on his chest. Reminiscent of the branding that is done by some fraternities, but I could tell that wasn't what it was. It was circular and small in diameter, but certainly not a birthmark. My curiosity was piqued; I wanted to be closer to it than just by simple touch. I licked along the side of the scar slowly with my tongue, and then alluringly kissed it.

"How did you get that?" I asked while still caressing the scar. My question was a routine mark of my inquisitive nature that was heightened by a genuine jealousy of everything that had the pleasure to be part of Kevin. --Scars and memories included.

Slowly removing his fingertips from their resting place of rubbing my hair, Kevin began to caress the scar himself and as if choosing his words carefully for both my ears and his own, he sighed and simply said, "Childhood injury."

"What happened?" As the words left my mouth I swear I could hear the small voice of a little devil propped up on my shoulder, whispering in my ear: "Curiosity killed the cat Kahla."

Kevin took a deep breath, and as he did so, somehow I knew deep within my being that what he was about to tell me was something he did not share often with others.

It was personal.

It was sacred.

I found joy in that possibility, that fact. But I was also nervous as to whether what he was about to relate would be something I wanted to hear or not. A mixture of joy at the closeness between us due to his opening up another side of him, combined with a fear that he would say something that would shatter my hopes of "happily ever after" engulfed me.

But the moment wasn't about me, even if I wanted and desired it to be.

He began to tell me his story.

"I was about 11 years old when a man broke into our house. Me, my sisters and my mother were all asleep at the time. Momma woke up to a man walking around in her bedroom rummaging through her jewelry box on top of her dresser. The little ballerina danced around in a circle as the song, "Isn't she lovely" played. The jewelry box was a gift to my mother from my grandmother before she died. It was my mother's most cherished possession. Sometimes she would sit in her room alone for hours and just listen to the music as the ballerina danced. Occasionally, she ran her finger up and down the figurine as it went round and round. I'm sure she was probably reliving some childhood memory that was the significance of the gift from her grandmother to her, but that is just conjecture on my part, as she never said as much.

The house was still and quiet except for the instrumental song being played. The sound of the music was the trigger to awaken my mother from her slumber and was the first indication my mother had of the intruder in the house. Momma did not believe in having guns in the house, but she knew she needed protection, so she kept a Louisville Slugger under her bed. She reached for the bat as she watched the robber grab her knickknacks from their resting place and put them by the handfuls into his pockets. Her motions to retrieve the bat from under the bed must have alerted the robber that she was awake and he lunged at her on her bed before she could get the bat for protection.

"Is this all you got? Where's the money bitch."

My mother screamed, "That's all I have, take it if you want to, and just leave me alone."

I think she screamed as loud as she did in an effort to wake me and my sisters up, as well as alert us that something was wrong and that we were to stay where we were. She wanted the robber to think that she was alone in the house. My sisters didn't even hear her scream and were still sound asleep in their bunk beds that lay adjacent to mine. But I heard her scream; I still hear it some nights. I was hard headed back then, just like I am now, so I immediately came running into her room. As I came in the door, I saw the man straddled over my mother on the bed, holding a knife to her throat.

"Bitch, don't play with me. Where's the money? Give it to me and I'll go with nobody getting hurt. Don't make me get ugly. You don't want to see me uglier than I am right now, so just give me yo' shit and I'm out!"

The look on his face as he spat the words out indicated he meant business. His voice was low and raspy, filled with desperation. I remembered being frozen in my tracks for a moment, asking myself, *is that dried up toothpaste around his mouth? Why do his lips have a dry white film around them and why are his eyes red as the tomatoes on the kitchen window sill?*

Momma was at the end of a knife, my two little sisters were still sleeping in the bedroom I shared with them, and we had no father figure around; so that left only me to do something. I had to be the one to change the fate of my family. That left me to save the day and stop the madness. Without a father figure around, that meant I was the man of the house, and that I had to protect the women. Even though I was only eleven, I knew what my role in the house was.—*To protect and serve.*

I wasn't armed with anything except my determination and courage…but they would have to do.

My eyes were bulging out of their sockets and anger took control. We didn't have much, hell, momma's jewelry was probably only worth $50, if that much, because most of it was costume. That's all she could afford on a waitress' salary to look good. But even though we didn't have much, what we did have was ours and I was determined to keep it that way. The fact that someone had the audacity to come in our home and try and take away things that belonged to my family made me feel I had the strength of Goliath and could kill anything and anyone with my bare hands if I had to. I remembered at the time, a show I had seen on TV where people had managed to demonstrate immeasurable and miraculous feats of strength when they needed to. Those people had turned over cars by themselves in order to rescue loved ones who were trapped beneath automobiles. As I psyched myself up to attack our attacker, I said to myself, *a crack-head robber is no match for me and I must protect momma.*

I ran through the threshold of the door toward the robber, screaming, "Leave my mother alone and get out of our house or I'll kill you."

I startled him. I don't think in his wildest dreams he expected an eleven year old to mess up his score. His eyes showed that he had bought my mother's ploy and thought that she lived in the house by herself. As I ran towards him, he swung the knife at me, missing on the upstroke but stabbing me on the down stroke. As the blade went into my chest, I remember stepping back in disbelief, holding the wound and frowning at the fact that I was bleeding. I fell to the floor and the blood began to pour out more rapidly. I still remember the warmth of the blood as it ran down my chest along the sides of my rib cage and form a puddle on the floor.

My momma was screaming louder. It was screeching and blood curdling. My sisters were alerted and called 911. As the sound of the sirens got closer, the robber decided to leave with what he had and he ran out the door.

Watching ambulances as they go down the street with the lights flashing as they break all rules of traffic in an attempt to save someone's life brings about certain emotions, mostly ones of irritation that you have to pull over to the side of the road to let them buy; but when you are on the inside of an ambulance, your thoughts turn to admiration at their efforts to save your life, as opposed to irritation at having to wait.

I was lucky. The knife hadn't hit any major arteries. I only received thirty four stitches and the scar is my constant reminder of my brush with death. I also got my fifteen minutes of fame since the story was all over KEYE evening news that night. They said I was a hero for protecting my mom.

I didn't feel like a hero. I was the man of the house, doing what the man of the house was supposed to do. What I had to do because there wasn't a real man around to do it for us."

Kevin got quiet for a moment and continued caressing his scar. His eyes looked sad, as if they had been transported in time back into the Twilight Zone. I squeezed his shoulders tighter and kissed his scar again.

"I had to grow up really fast to fill the void of a father in our home. My childhood was robbed from me and I vowed my children would grow up with both parents in their home. I would never abandon an offspring of mine like my dad had abandoned us.--NEVER!" He placed extreme emphasis on that last word.

Kevin began running his hands through my hair again, and placed his nose closer to me, inhaling my scalp and forehead. Then he cupped his hands around my face and kissed me. As he probed his tongue in and out of my mouth the wetness and the warmth of his kisses lulled me, capturing every sensor in my body from my eyelids to my big toe. He was kissing my mouth, yet my toes began to curl.

As our lips parted, Kevin looked me deep in the eyes and said, "I could kiss you all day. I can't get enough of having my mouth inside yours. This is what a kiss is supposed to feel like."

Kevin told me that kisses with his wife were not like kisses with me. He said that they did the "married people" kiss. He explained that married people kiss every morning, usually a light peck on the cheek, forehead, or lips as they are walking out of the door and saying goodbye for the day. They say, "I love you," which is what they feel, only not quite. They do love each other, but they are not really "in love" with each other. Time snatched the deepness of that feeling from the marriage. Both the kiss and the comment were mundane, robotic and routine. There was no passion, just obligation to do and say it. It was automatic just like a morning shower and cup of coffee. There was no thought or desire attached or motivating the kiss, just an automatic reflex to deliver it.

Kevin said that the same was true to him and Nicole's sex life. He went on to say that after years of marriage, sex had become a perfunctory and obligatory action. If one partner wanted it, the other obliged. Both partners knew where to touch the other to get the other to the point of climax. He touched here, she touched there, and then they move into the positions that they know will produce the desired result. It was a sexual game of *Twister*. There was very little excitement, no newness and no goose bumps, --just routine, mundane actions.

It was not like that with us.

When Kevin and I made love, our bodies formed a beautiful picture, alive with vibrant colors; a mold of ecstasy and passion oozing out of every pore of our skin. I could not get enough of Kevin. I was not simply kissing him all over, I was devouring him. His skin was an aphrodisiac to me. I loved the way his skin smelled, looked and tasted. The more I tasted it, the more I had to have. I couldn't stop nibbling, biting and sucking every inch of his dark chocolate skin. And I just couldn't seem to satisfy my craving for him.

Kevin's actions suggested he could not get enough of me either. My neck and chest were proof positive of his insationable lust for my skin. I had passion marks all over me. Man, it had been a long time since I had those marks, or felt the feeling that comes along with receiving them; you know, that "hurt so good feeling." I had been more careful on him. Even in the heat of passion, I was conscious of the fact that he was not mine, and that passion marks would cause problems for him and for us, so I resisted my natural urge to mark my territory like a dog peeing on a tree. I must admit stifling my desire to use my teeth and nails to tear into his skin, really turned me on. I couldn't remember a time when my nipples were as hard as they were that night. Our first encounter, which was initiated in my kitchen, had led to several more encounters in my bedroom that night.

I've had several lovers in my lifetime, but none like Kevin. None of them were as passionate; none of them were able to make my body quiver like he had. I had never had as many orgasms as I did that night. If Kevin were pulling out all the stops to make me hooked, he had done a good job, because I was in; hook, line and sinker. This had to be the feeling that gets junkies hooked off their very first hit of any drug. Kevin was liquid crack for me and I wanted to scream, "Hit me again bartender." I was intoxicated from him. My body craved another hit, and another and another. His loving was in my veins.

Maybe it was so good to me because I hadn't had sex in a long time.

Maybe it was so good because of all the taunting and teasing we had done to each other.

Maybe it was so good because I knew he could never be mine and he was the "forbidden fruit."

Whatever the reason was, all I knew was; the loving was good.

But reality hit me hard like a ton of bricks falling on my head the next morning. Even though I had experienced passion; even though parts of my body were more alive than they had ever been before; even though he had awakened parts of me that I did not know existed; let alone knew were asleep, and even though the night before felt so good and so right, the end result was the same. I was still waking up in my bed ALONE.

My lover, my prince charming, my passionate confidant was; after all--married.

At three in the morning, he had left my bed to go home to what really mattered to him. His wife. I had to deal with that. Whether I liked it or not, that fact was being shoved in my face and down my throat, like cold medicine or Castor Oil to a sick child who doesn't want to take it.

Mistress Memoirs

I had to take a back seat to his wife, and somehow, the emptiness of my bed was worse on that day. It was worse because I had tasted a delicacy that I wanted but could not have; worse because for the entire night, Kevin professed his love for me; worse because he stated to me over and over how good I made him feel. In one word, I was "amazing." Those were his words; that's what he said. He continued his sentiment by saying he never had felt so alive with anyone, not in the same way he felt when he was with me.

That made it worse. Worse because even if the things he said to me were really what he was feeling, it all boiled down to the fact that he was still hers, bottom line. I was just sharing, having an appetizer, a mere taste of his world. He had left me, and the bed we made love in over and over again, to return to her. – *Wifey*, and I was nothing more than a sloppy second to her.

It was the morning after and I was in the same situation I was in the day before.

I still had my good job, my nice car, my big house with the big bed decorated with expensive satin sheets and throw pillows. Yet after a heated night of passion, which had warmed my soul and my bed, I was abandoned by my lover and that same bed took on the characteristics that it had before…back to how it had always been – cold and lonely.

Tangled Temptation

It was Saturday morning and I awoke up alone to the warm rays from the sun coming in through the bay windows of my bedroom. The curtains were blowing in the wind and for a moment I lay in my bed reflecting on the events of the night before, recognizing that I couldn't sleep my problems away. I made myself get out of the bed and I walked over to the balcony, opened the doors and as I looked out into my yard at the flowers beginning to bloom, I felt a deeper level of loneliness than I had ever experienced before. The sorrowful thoughts I had the night before, moved from remorse and sadness; to a position of straight up anger. All the thoughts of me ruining Kevin's happy home transformed to me putting the blame back on Kevin where it belonged. He was the culprit. He was the one doing wrong, not me. I could not ruin his home, only he and his wife were capable of bringing about that ending. That union was owned by the two of them and only they could sell it or give it away.

Lorraine Elzia

I told myself that I was NOT the one who took marital vows before God and professed that I would be with someone for the rest of my life. I was NOT the one who said, "For better or worse, till death do us part."

I was NOT the guilty party; he was.

He was the one that was lying to both of us.

He was lying to his wife daily, telling her he was at work, all the while he was spending time with me. In turn, he was lying to me by saying that he loved and cared for me, all the while he just wanted to have his cake and eat it too. If he really loved me, he would not have left my bed at the wee hours of the morning. The goodbye kiss he gave me would not have been enough for him.

If he loved me, he would still be in my bed with me trying to determine how he was going to tell *her* that he had found the love of his life and what they once had was over.

In reality, I knew it was not that simple.

I knew it was not that cut and dry.

But I don't always live in reality. Who does?

At that moment of being alone, instead of choosing to be sad and lonely, I resolved to be angry with him. My head was spinning and as I looked around, so was my bedroom. My eyes were bloodshot red, puffy from crying and my head began to ache. I may have been putting more into it than I should have, but I couldn't stop. I needed some help.

Now one thing that should be understood about me is that I am a very private person. I have friends, and associates, but I am not the type of person that sits and tells her girlfriends all the things of her personal life.

If Kevin had done his homework as thoroughly as I assumed he had, maybe that was part of the reason he choose me. I was a safe target...too smart to lower myself into becoming a stalker; and too private a person to put his business, or mine for that matter, out in the streets.

Although I trusted my girls not to spread my business, you never can tell. I was a firm believer of the saying, "better safe than sorry." So I just kept my private life private. Which, in the scheme of things was easy to do when you spend most of your days alone, not talking to anyone. Opening up and relating a feeling to others was more alien to me than retreating within myself for comfort.

As I sat there with fumes of anger coming off my head, I wanted to call a friend, cry and ask for advice. I needed some girlfriend time. I needed one of my friends to listen and tell me what to do. But I was a foreigner in that territory. Crying over a man was new to me, and I was too proud, to share that with others. So I had to deal with it, like I dealt with everything else in my life, alone and without help.

"So, Kahla, you slipped. You had an error in judgment. It happens. Even to the best of us." My mind said. *"But you are back now."*

I realized I was too intelligent to let the affair continue. I would stop it; stop it right there. I knew I was on an emotional roller coaster, so I knew I needed to slow it all down and think. I knew I had to wait until I was stronger.

Up to that point all I had engaged in was just a one-night stand. – a booty call with benefits. I was determined not to let it become more than that. I was on a mission that it would not become an affair.

"I deserve more than half a man." I told myself.

"I deserve my own man."

But the question before me was; could I say that decisive statement to Kevin? Hell yeah, I could; just not right at that moment. I said out loud to myself. I needed some time. Time to gather my thoughts on what I would say; and exactly how I would say it. I was an emotional train wreck, so I knew I didn't have the strength to do it then; I'd have to wait until I was stronger.

I knew how to blow off the players, the derelicts, the losers and the abusers; the ones I didn't care for. But I didn't know how to blow off someone I loved.

I decided my game plan would be to avoid him for a while, just until I could get my bearings; my thoughts in order. --Until I was stronger.

No calls, no lunches, no emails, and definitely under no circumstance would I see him.

I knew I was much stronger when I was not in his presence.

When I was not caught up under the glare of his mesmerizing eyes.

"Yeah, I just needed to wait until I was stronger, until the power of those eyes of his had lost some of their magnetic hold on me. That's my game plan." I told myself.

"No contact."

And then it began. The phone rang. I listened to it.... ring, ring, ring. Without looking at the caller ID I knew it was him. I swear my phone rang differently when it was Kevin. As much as my heart wanted to answer it and hear his voice, my head would not allow it.

Then I heard my answering machine, "You've reached Kahla, at the tone, you know what to do," beep.

"Kahla, Kahla, you there?

Instant Goosebumps again, damn why did the sound of his voice cause that reaction? I began to think of the study done by the Russian Physiologist, Ivan Pavlov, in which he was able to make a dog salivate at the mere sound of a bell ringing, without the dog even seeing food.

It was a conditioned response. A simple study of cause and reaction; it showed how conditioning could cause a certain reaction, a certain response. That is what was going on with Kevin and me. Just his voice caused me to salivate from more than one body orifice.

"Kahla, last night was wonderful. I miss you baby. Call me when you get home, I need you." He had a lonely pang in his voice.

"You need me?"

"You need me!!!"

My anger level was rising to the point of steam coming out of a boiling tea kettle on a hot stove burner.

"If you needed me, why did you leave this morning? If you needed me, you would be here with me right now, not on the other end of the phone. No, man, you don't need me; you need your damn wife. That's who you need. You proved that when you left MY damn bed this morning. Actions speak louder than words, and your actions show you need HER not ME!"

Mistress Memoirs

I realized I was screaming at the answering machine and not the object of my anger —Kevin. But I was too chicken shit to lift up the receiver and say those things to him. It felt good hollering them at my machine nonetheless...even if he didn't hear what I was thinking, at least the words were being said, even if no one was hearing them; they had jumped ship from out of my head.

Thirty minutes later another call, then another, and another one after that. Each call stated how much he cared, how much he wanted to see me, needed to see me, and how he was getting worried because I wasn't answering my home phone or my cell.

I couldn't talk to him, not then, and at the time I thought, probably not ever.

I continued to ignore his calls, existing in a haze, lounging around in my pajamas all day in a funk, watching Saturday afternoon made-for-TV movies on my flat screen plaza TV and eating Rocky Road Hagen Daas Ice Cream; you know, the usual depression routine. Somehow, watching a movie about someone else's tragic life always seemed to make me feel better about my own.

As I lost myself in the movie, and began rooting for the battered wife on the screen who was burning her husband's clothes and setting their house on fire as she drove off feeling vindicated; my doorbell rang.

I grabbed my robe and walked down the stairs. When I was about three steps from the bottom, I could see his silhouette through the frosted glass door. I paused and I swore my heart skipped a beat or two.

"Damn, how am I supposed to stick to my game plan when this man won't play by the damn rules?" I asked myself.

Knock Knock.

"Kahla, Kahla it's me." I stood on step three paralyzed as if frozen in time.

"Kahla, are you okay?"

I didn't want to move, but he was yelling loudly and I had to shut him up. What would my siddity-ass neighbors think of the scene he was causing? He must have thought he was at the doors of the Cabrini Greens Projects, instead of my Suburban Township.

Kah.... I opened the door mid sentence.

"It's about time girl, you had me worried."

I just stared at him.

He flashed his pearly whites at me, "Are you gonna let me in?" He said as he leaned forward to kiss me.

He was dressed in his uniform and looking good as usual. Flashbacks of his gun belt hitting the floor along with his pants the night before invaded my mind.

"Don't do that Kevin, and I really don't think your coming inside my house is a good idea right now." I raised my hand to the middle of his chest to stop him dead in his tracks.

"Kahla, what's wrong? After last night this is the response I get, come on, let me in honey, and tell me what's wrong."

"Last night is what's wrong, and I'm just not feeling up to company right now. I'll call you Kevin." I turned to walk away, but Kevin pushed his way in and closed the door behind him. He grabbed me and I was literally and figuratively caught in a tailspin.

"Kahla, talk to me. Tell me what's wrong baby. I've been thinking about you all day. I've been calling you and you don't answer. Talk to me. Kahla, just talk to me."

I looked into his eyes and thought it was too soon for that shit. I wasn't ready. I wasn't strong enough yet, not at that time. But whether I liked it or not, it was happening, right then, and I had to deal with it.

I needed to arm myself for the battle at hand. I took a mental inventory of the relationship ending weapons that are normally a part of a woman's arsenal; you know, tears, hollering, throwing things, or simply just being a bitch.

I decided against using all of those and opted for my selected weapons of choice; which were sarcasm and guilt.

Grabbing Kevin's strong manly hand and cupping it within my own freshly manicured hands, I lead him away from the front door, through the foyer, into the living room and over to the couch.

"That's more like it girl. Did you miss me too? Show daddy some love." He grimaced with a self-righteous grin.

"Forgive me honey, I sure did. Tell me about your day," I said sweetly while feigning interest in his bull-shit conversation, as we both got comfortable.

"Whew." He exhaled, letting out a sigh that was evidence of a long day. Kevin leaned back into the plush oversized pillows that permeated my sofa couch, while putting his feet up on my ottoman as he closed his eyes.

How dare he be so comfortable in MY home, when he had already walked in and turned my life upside down? I thought to myself as I tried to hide the fact that I was rolling my eyes at his nonchalant recognition of the situation at hand, coupled with his macho audacity.

He needed to catch a clue.

But of course…he didn't.

"Today was long baby girl. They really expect a brotha to work these days for a paycheck, how fair is that?" He said with a chuckle, "And damn, a brotha was already tired after that loving you whipped out on me last night. You've really got some skills girl; I'll give you that."

He grinned, still keeping his eyes closed and resting his head on my shoulders.

Clueless! I thought to myself.

I put my arms around his head and began massaging his temples, all the while really wanting to ring his freaking neck!

"I'm sorry your day was hard baby." I said as I nibbled on his ear, probing and flickering my tongue in and out of it in a way I knew would drive him wild and ending with a light sucking of the lobe.

"So does wifey know you're here right now; or does she think you're out defending the streets of Chicago?

I uttered my remark, knowing my sarcastic comment would make him uneasy and piss him the hell off. I got joy in having the upper hand.

But in usual Eckhart style….Kevin flipped the script on me.

"Why are you starting with that shit Kahla? Is that what's been bothering you all day today? My fucking marital state? Is that why you have been avoiding me? All of a sudden my marriage is a problem for you?" He chuckled, sucked on his teeth, looked at me from the ground up as if surveying my worth and continued on.

"Hump, it's funny that whether I was married or not didn't seem to bother yo' ass too much last night when I was tapping that ass and you were grabbing the headboard and screaming out my name."

He tilted his head back, closed his eyes and mimicked me from the night before. "Oh Kevin, don't stop baby, don't stop!"

Whew!!! I thought to myself. That was a low blow if ever I heard one.

A sucker punch as they call it on the streets.

I felt that cut way down deep, and decided the weapon of choice for that assault would be physical.

A beat down was both imminent and necessary!

I slowly removed my hands from his temples and rose up off the couch and replaced them with a hard slap across his face as hard as I possibly could. I hit him so hard I heard the sound echoing over and over, sort of like a yodel belched out from a mountaintop by a Swiss maiden with long braided ponytails and an ugly dress. I still don't know if the echo was reality or if it was just my mind's way of reliving the slap over and over again.

Momentary justification is what I felt.

A jubilant grin became a squatter on my face.

He cupped his jaw in the palm of his hand and slowly looked up at me. I got an adrenaline rush, as anger mixed with fear ran through my veins. I braced myself for physical retaliation, but instead of hitting me back, Kevin stared at me with hurt puppy dog eyes and said, "You know what? It's a good thing I don't hit women. What is your problem Kahla? You're tripping about my wife, but what's she got to do with OUR thang? I love you. Don't I show it? I make you as big a part of my life as I possibly can. My life was missing something before I met you. I've never felt like this before. Don't take that feeling away.

What do you want from me? I love you; tell me how to make it right."

"What do I want?" I rolled my eyes in disgust at his ignorance.

"What do I want from you, Kevin?" My vehement scream was deafening to even my own ears.

"Yes, tell me what you want." His appeal was earnest and humble.

I lowered my eyes and my voice. Pathetically, I tried to answer his question through my frustration.

"I want it ALL Kevin. Can you give me that? Well, CAN YOU Kevin?"

A stupid stare was his answer as I continued on with my tirade. I felt my head rolling uncontrollably in "sista girl" style for effect as I emphasized each word.

"I want ALL the things you are giving to her Kevin. ALL the things SHE has. I want ALL your time, ALL your attention, and ALL your love. Not the fifty percent you give me now. Call me selfish if you like Kevin, but I want ALL of you. I don't think that's too much to ask...I want ALL of you, that's ALL I want!"

The waterworks had started, and I couldn't stop the flow. Niagara Falls had nothing on my tear glands. I tasted the salty fluid as it ran across my lips and dripped off my chin.

I guess the production number I had just displayed for him had finally enlightened Kevin to the severity of the situation.

There were no words from him in response.

No macho colloquy, no arguments or pleas for consideration.

Just warm strong arms engulfing me, hugging me deep.

I did not resist.

He ran his fingers through my hair, as I felt my body become less stringent to his touch. I fought the underlying tendency to slacken my resistance.

"I can't do this Kevin," I uttered. "I need and deserve more."

Kevin wiped the tears from my eyes and let his fingers lingered on my cheeks. "You certainly do, and no truer words have ever been spoken. I'll fix it Kahla, just give me some time, and I'll fix it. I need you girl. I really do. I didn't realize it before I got to know you, but now that I have you in my life; I see that I can't go on living unless you are a part of my world."

Soft lips invaded my eyelids with butterfly kisses; followed by sensuous pecks to my nose, cheeks and finally my lips. His breath was hot, sweet, and inviting.

My guard was not only down; it had all but evaporated and disappeared.

"Just give me some time, baby girl; that's all I need; just a little more time to figure it all out; time to make it work. You want ALL of me, and that's what I want to give you. Just don't cut me off, not now, not ever. You'll have ALL of me, Kahla, I promise you that, because I know I have to surrender myself to you in order to feel whole, I am nothing without you."

His words soothed me. They were probably a crock of shit and I knew that, but I truly felt comfort in hearing them from my lover's lips.

I desperately wanted to believe him.

I needed to believe him.

I had to believe him for my own mental sanity and well being; so I did.

I relinquished my anger.

Recognizing I couldn't fight the battle of his marital situation at that time. I didn't want to be his adversary in the love game. That wouldn't advance my cause at all.

I needed to win the war.

In order to do that, I felt that I could get closer to him and his heart if I were an Ally; a soldier down for the cause.

Lulling in his soothing arms, I forgot the fact that I was angry; I forgot the fact that I needed to correct the mistake of the night before and end the affair. Instead, I looked in his eyes and was hypnotized and I bought was he was selling as I let my lips be the ones to initiate the "seek and find" mission that time.

Cum Correct

I just want to be cumming

in a slow grind,

moving in unison

with one another

erotic energy

breathing hard

juices flowing

I want to be cumming

No need for candles,

music or a slow beat

hit it from the back,

against a wall

Fuck getting under them sheets

I wanna be cumming

Spank me

kiss me

bite me as well

let me stroke you

and suck you

and make you swell

I NEED to scream out "Hell Yeah"!!!!

Lorraine Elzia

I wanna be cumming

I'll rub my clit

pleasure myself

you can join if you want to

Toys, gels and even your finger will do

I just want to be cumming

I just want to cum

multiple times till I'm sloppy wet

eye's rolling

back arching

skin tasting

of all I can get

I just want to be cumming

I need to be cumming

OVER AND OVER again cumming

and I want to be cumming with you.

Kahla

And Justice For All

Prosecutor Samuel Lovett was deep into his cross-examination of Lionel Walker, a two-strike convicted criminal, working on his third strike before being told "you're out." Criminals, who had several felony convictions for the same offense, were prosecuted by the District Attorney's Office under the "Three Strikes" program. If convicted a third time, they would automatically receive a life sentence for their crime. Under the program, repeat offenders got bumped up to the front of the punishment line, so to speak, Chicago style.

Lionel had been tried and convicted twice before for Indecent Assault on a child. His first crime was against his thirteen-year old step-daughter for repeated sexual abuse over a three-year time frame in which he forced her to perform oral sex on him in exchange for a ride home from school so she didn't have to take the crowded, urine smelling L-train from her school in the suburbs to her house in the projects. The young girl only wanted a chance at a better education and she told herself that sucking Lionel's dick everyday was her cross to bear for wanting the dream of graduating from a respectable school on the "right" side of town. What started out as blow jobs progressed to full sex as Lionel's desires took control.

The story only came to light when the victim had to inform her mother that she was pregnant and the added salt to an open wound of who the father was. Needless to say, the mother couldn't get to the police station fast enough to have Lionel's ass locked up. Love is one thing, protection of bear cubs by momma bear is another. Too bad more mothers don't recognize that rule of thumb.

Lionel opted for a Bench Trial instead of a trial before a jury, and the judge in his case gave him a measly eight years for deflowering the young girl and fathering an offspring with her. With "good behavior" while in jail, his time only amounted to four years.

Side note: I never understood the term "good behavior" concerning those in prison. When your meals, self containment, safety and very existence are all contingent upon your ability to follow the rules and play nicely without being put in time out...well, that's not "good behavior"...that's SURVIVAL. – An instinct that is innate in all animals. Do what you need to do in order to survive...by any means necessary. That's the mentality. Very little restraint and control are involved in that; just a desire to survive and do whatever is necessary to accomplish that goal. Why we, as a society have missed the mark on that one and seem to reward actions of prisoners to survive in an environment that they placed themselves in because of their own destructive behavior, is beyond my comprehension. – But I digress.

Good behavior or survival; call it what you will; Lionel had mastered it that very first jail term and was released early.

Mistress Memoirs

It only took two months of being back on the streets before Lionel was back to his old tricks and began patrolling for a new victim, whom he found at the middle school that hired him as part of the maintenance staff. Lionel was an indiscriminate and equal opportunistic rapist. He didn't care about the sex of the child as long as sex with a child was what he was getting.

His second victim, a young boy of twelve, said that while Lionel was penetrating him he seemed to say over and over in chant-like form, "A hole is a hole...long as I can fill it...its all good and it's all the same."

Years later, when the case finally made it to court, while on the witness stand, the boy would state how that statement, more than the act itself, degraded him most. In his mind, the words uttered to him in the middle of the raping of his body, — raped his mind and his manhood as well.

"A hole is a hole," the boy would later repeat over and over while rolling his eyes and crying uncontrollably while testifying.

"A HOLE IS A HOLE. To me that meant I wasn't a boy, I wasn't a man, I wasn't a female, I was nothing more than a mere toilet in which he urinated his sperm into. I wasn't even human. I was an object. Nothing more than a portal for his backed-up blue ball releases. I don't think I will ever understand the "why" of that." The boy's eyes indicated to all who saw them that he was in a perpetual state of trying to make sense of what happened to him at Lionel's hands. He was wise beyond his years, yet irreconcilably damaged.

That boy...
        that statement...
    sealed Lionel's fate.

At least in the minds of the jurors in his trial.

Unlike the judge in the first trial, his second time around yielded a much harder sentence for Lionel and his punishment was twenty years. But being a master of working the judicial system, Lionel only served nine years after receiving leniency for "good behavior" and time served while locked up awaiting trial.

Within a year of being released from jail the second time, Lionel committed his third crime, which was the basis of my chance encounter with him. Lionel's case was assigned to our court before the Honorable Lucas McCormick or "Iron hand Luke" as he was called by all those that had the unfortunate experience of having received punishment at his hands. Lionel was charged with the brutal kidnapping and continuous sexual assault of two sixteen-year old girls from Covington High School. He met the girls at a bus stop outside the mall, struck up conversation, and agreed to give them a ride home. But "home" was not the destination he had in mind.

Maybe it was his sensible, middle-aged looks that made the girls comfortable enough to get in his car. He did have a father-like appearance about him.

Maybe it was the fact that the girls found a false sense of security in the fact that there were two of them; safety in numbers, which might have made them feel invincible to a potential predator.

Maybe it was a belief that terrible things happened to other people and couldn't possibly happen to them.

Maybe they believed that all the stories in the newspapers about sexual assaults happened to bad girls; other girls; not to girls like them.

Whatever the reason for the lowering of their guard, Lionel offered the ride and they accepted.

The charges brought against Lionel by the State were that once both girls were in his car, Lionel put a gun to the temple of one of the girls who was sitting upfront with him in the passenger seat. He threatened to kill them both if they did not cooperate. He took them to his house, chained the girls by their ankles in his basement and over a four-day period continually raped each girl, one right after the other, over and over again at his leisure. He seemed to be the poster child for erectile stability. Viagra had nothing on Lionel's libido.

His reign of sexual terror over the young girls came to an end when one of them was able to grab Lionel's phone while he was asleep and send a text message to her father of their whereabouts.

Mistress Memoirs

At his arraignment, Lionel plead not guilty. A trial ensued and he testified in his own defense before "Iron Hand Luke." In his defense, Lionel insisted that the girls had not told him their real ages and that they were willing, and consensual participants in a weekend sexual bondage fantasy shared by all three of them; a *threesome with benefits*, as he described it.

We were two weeks into the trial, and on day three of cross examination by Mr. Lovett, when my mind began to wander as the prosecutor and defendant went round and round about the semantics of consent of the girls.

All the mentioning of sex and consent and bondage had taken my mind back to my encounters with Kevin and I began creating new scenarios in my head of bondage games we could play.

Humph, I wonder if 'Cum and Play,' the adult toy store down on 67th carries handcuffs. I thought to myself.

First I allowed myself to indulge in sexual fantasies with me and Kevin as role-play actors in scenes from that of Little Red Riding Hood and the Big Bad Wolf; to another scene of Kevin as a bed-ridden patient in a hospital receiving a sponge bath from me, his naughty nurse. My mind initially enjoyed the role play and ran with the possibilities; but that was short lived. In the hospital scenario, it ended with his wife coming in while I was in the middle of lathering him up. That reminder of Kevin's marital status injected in the middle of my fantasy, instantly shifted my mind to our argument the night before and my pleas to have Kevin as my own. I wanted to slap myself for being so vulnerable to him. For letting him have control over me and allowing him to know that I was weak when it came to him.

I got butterflies in the pit of my stomach. Well, it felt like butterflies, but was more than likely just acid indigestion--a result of not being able to stomach or digest my own actions; my feelings for Kevin, and irritation and shame with how I had acted in letting him see the vulnerability that resided in me. My stomach was showing disgust for the *taste* of the whole situation. I was in a state of reliving and *regurgitating* the error of letting Kevin in my life to begin with.

I was watching the reenactment of the events of the two days prior over and over again in my head and shaking my head in disbelief at all that I had done and said. I assumed I had only been distracted for a hot minute with those thoughts, but in hindsight, I realized that I had been in a fantasy land of my own, consumed with Kevin and his hold on me for longer than I had initially thought. While I was frolicking around with the thoughts in my head, doing the nasty with Kevin and rewinding our argument; a heated moment had occurred in the courtroom.

One of great significance; I hadn't noticed it brewing because I had drifted off mentally and missed the whole thing. While I was in Lala land, imagining myself laid out in the woods in my Little Red Riding Hood getup screaming, *"Eat me Big Bad Wolf...Eat me just like you said you would,"* I was clearly clueless as to what was going on around me in the courtroom. I was oblivious to my surroundings and what was going on...oblivious to anything that was outside of my fantasy of Kevin orally pleasing me while dressed as a wolf, and at that moment, what was going on in the courtroom did not matter; only being an entree' did.

My moment of return from the Twilight Zone occurred when I heard Iron Hand Luke say,

"Counsel, enough of the arguing. For

clarification purposes as to whether Mr.

Walker, has in fact, actually confessed here

on the witness stand in open court to the

charges against him as stated by the

prosecution; or if he was merely indicating

a hypothetical speculation of what MIGHT

happen as indicated in the Motion for

Dismissal argued by the defense; I will refer

to the exact language from Mr. Walker's

mouth and will take the matter under

advisement before making my ruling. I'll

listen to the exact verbal testimony of Mr.

Walker, interpret it, and make my decision

with respect to the law accordingly. Will the

Court Reporter please read back the

testimony of the last four questions and

answers in the cross examination of Mr.

Walker by Mr. Lovett."

As if the volume in the courtroom were turned up on my mental television, I was suddenly shocked back to the moment at hand and realized that all eyes in the courtroom were on me. Every seat in the courtroom was taken and had been for weeks. That fact, coupled with the media cameras in each corner of the courtroom and reporters along the back near the door, left no room for another body in the room. It was more packed in there than *standing room only*; there was barely breathing room in Iron Hand Luke's domain. As he ordered me to read back the testimony, you could hear a pin drop and I felt a single drop of sweat roll down the small of my back from the extreme tension in the courtroom.

"Yes, Your Honor."

I said the acknowledgement of his request confidently as I always had when asked to read back in court. Court Reporters are the official voice of the court and are often asked -- when there is a dispute or question concerning testimony -- to read the verbatim words spoken by the parties in trial. It comes with the territory of the job to be put on the spot often, especially in high-profile cases, so it was nothing new to me. I had done it thousands of times without blinking an eye.

But this time was different; very different.

As I glanced down and began to grab the paper transcript from my steno machine to read the testimony, I saw that there was nothing there. No keystrokes, no shorthand words, no ink, no nothing.

Lorraine Elzia

I hadn't taken down a single word since the beginning of the day's events. My moment of escaping into Kevin-land; a place of both tranquility and pain; had caused me to neglect my job and my duty as an officer of the court.

"Oh Shit!" I screamed inside my head.

"Ms. Thompson, is there a problem?" The judge seemed irritated at me being the pause in his proceedings.

"Ms. Thompson, just start at the beginning of this line of questioning, you don't have to look for the exact question, just go to beginning of the exchange." He thought he was helping me. But there was no help for me in sight. I didn't have ANY of the testimony – not the beginning, the middle or the end.

I began to curse myself that I had not used a tape recorder as a backup like so many other reporters did. I had never used one in my career because I thought that the use of electronic equipment to take down testimony was cheating on my job and lessened my confidence in myself and my capabilities.

I thought it lessened the profession.

Besides, if I were a court reporter worth my certification, my skills on my steno machine were all that was needed. If a court could just tape record what was being said, why was there a need for me? That was my rationale. I made it a point not to use recordings as a means of doing my part for job security for my profession as a whole. Some reporters use them as a backup, I chose not to. At that moment, I wished I had not been so self-righteous in my own abilities and had *cheated*, as I called it, by using the aid of electronics.

"We're waiting Ms. Thompson."

I took a deep breath and prepared myself for the inevitable. I knew the extent of the damage the words I had to say would have.

"Judge McCormick, I am embarrassed to admit this, but I won't be able to read back that portion of the testimony. As a matter of fact, respectfully sir, I don't have any of the testimony since we began."

"Excuse me Ms. Thompson. Did you say you don't have ANY of the testimony?"

"Yes, Sir. I have no excuse. I can only say that it seems like I was distracted for awhile."

"Distracted? Is that what you call it Ms. Thompson? You have jeopardized this whole trial and all you can give me as an excuse is the word, "distracted?" Iron Hand Luke looked like he wanted to show me the reason his name was given to him.

The Defense Attorney's eyes popped and he jumped to his feet as if he were a kernel of corn in one of those Jiffy Pop Corn stove-top poppers. "Your Honor, on behalf of my client, Lionel Walker, I move for a Mistrial for procedural error."

Mr. Lovett jumped up as well. Mid-air he seemed to snarl at me in disdain. "Your Honor, the State has spent over a million dollars in preparation, man hours, and pursuit of trying of this case. The taxpayers of this county deserve justice for Mr. Walker's actions and their money spent in attempt to punish him for his crimes. A mistrial is not in the best interest of society, in general, nor the State as a whole. We cannot afford to retry this case, and the State respectfully asks that you deny the Defense's motion for Mistrial."

"Ms. Thompson and Counsel, in my Chambers now! We stand in recess." Iron Hand Luke hit his gavel down so hard that I think the gavel cracked, and if it didn't, it sure sounded like it did.

I slowly moved from behind my steno machine and knew I was up shit's creek without a paddle. As the judge walked down from the bench, you could feel his anger and almost see a puff of smoke behind him. The Defense attorney had a skip in his step, child-like in nature as he followed the judge. He looked happier than a cat that had just swallowed a rat. It was apparent that he knew he had a chance at victory and freedom for his client. A chance, that but for my error, did not exist before. Mr. Lovett walked to chambers as well, grabbing law books with each arm as he did. It was apparent he was hoping to find some section of the law in the next few seconds that would help cover his ass and put a halt to what we all knew was destined to happen.

There was a murmur and grumbling in the courtroom as trial spectators gasped and gossiped about what would happen next. Cameras flashed all around me and some of the reporters jetted out the door hoping to get the story to their newsrooms before anyone else, so that they could air the story first.

What a way to get my fifteen minutes of fame. I shook my head in disbelief at my situation.

I was the last to go into the judge's chamber. As I walked inside, I slowly closed the door behind me and took a deep breath as I sat in the only chair left in the room. Judge McCormick's chambers were on the left side of the courthouse facing to the East. He kept the large, heavy, rustic wood-stained blinds closed tightly to avoid the sun. The gloominess of his chambers was fitting for the situation at hand. Behind his desk were two large book cases that held impressive law books with pictures of his family sprinkled in as book ends. Judge McCormick was seated with his back to us in a black leather, high-back, swivel chair. There was nothing but silence in the room as he seemed to stare aimlessly at the law books facing him. Without turning around he said, "Ms. Thompson, we have worked together for over eight years, this is unlike you. Would you care to explain yourself?"

I thanked God for his mercy that I did not have to look in the eyes of Iron Hand Luke. The eyes of disappointment from someone you admire can pierce your soul much more than any physical punishment.

"Respectfully, Your Honor, I honestly don't know what happened. I have no excuse and can only offer my apology." I looked at the floor as I nervously answered him, hoping he would chew me out later instead of in ear shot of the lawyers.

The room fell silent again for a few moments and then the Defense Attorney decided he would seize the moment and began to plead his case. Lionel's attorney was a short, balding, sloppy looking man. His suits always looked like they needed to be ironed and his shoes looked like he had shined them with a Hershey's bar. At first glance, one would think that he was in over his head with Lionel's case since he always had a look of confusion on his face whenever anything was said. But for the first time in the trial, he seemed to be smug. An air of confidence surrounded him that he had not had a couple of hours before. He almost seemed taller as he began to speak.

"Your Honor, I know this is a difficult situation, but the law is pretty cut and dry here. In a trial of this magnitude, where the defendant faces life in prison, it is more important than in other trials for there to be an accurate record. The fact that Ms. Thompson has failed to keep an accurate record infringes on the rights of my client –Rights afforded to him under the Constitution which you have a duty to make sure he receives. Let's say for the sake of argument that my client was found guilty at the end of this trial, without a record of what was said in open court, we would have no concrete evidence to use as a basis for an appeal; and the ability to appeal is crucial for someone who faces a life sentence. The failure on the part of your court reporter to accurately record the trial, not only affects this trial and its outcome, but it affects my client's appellate rights should the need arise to appeal. Mr. Walker's freedom should not be in jeopardy based solely upon the recollections in the minds of jurors, counsel, or even the judge himself. My client's freedom should be based solely on the facts presented in trial and without a record; we have no supporting evidence of what those facts were. You cannot allow his freedom to be taken away from him without a verbatim record of these proceedings. Without a record, there can always be speculation as to what was said in the trial. While it is unfortunate that Ms. Thompson's actions are the basis for a mistrial, there really can be no other outcome to these proceedings than for you to declare a mistrial for procedural error."

"Mr. Lovett, would you like to make an argument to the motion of opposing counsel?" The judge vehemently spit out the words with his back still to all of us.

Mr. Lovett flipped through a few pages in the law book in his hand and then seemed to exhale with disgust at the fact that even he had to admit that he would not be able to find salvation for his case in a matter of seconds. You could smell desperation in his breath as he said, "Your Honor, I will restate my argument as stated earlier; the State has spent a lot of time and effort in trying this case. The people of Chicago cannot afford to try this case again, so if you rule in favor of a mistrial, you will be letting a guilty man go free; not based on lack of evidence, not based on innocence, but based upon the error of your court staff. All of the efforts of the police department, detectives and the attorneys in this case will have all been a total waste of time. Allowing Mr. Walker to walk based upon the error of your reporter will basically be a slap in the face to the victims and their families. The victims are two young girls who were physically, mentally and emotionally scarred for life. How can you let them feel that their torture and their pursuit of punishing the man who did it was a waste of time? Those two girls, their families and the taxpayers of this State are entitled to more justice than that. It was apparent that we were on our way to proving this man guilty as charged. To rob these families of the opportunity of seeing him go to jail based solely on the actions of your staff is unfair and unjust."

Iron Hand Luke leaned back in his chair as far as it could go, then he swung around facing us for the first time since we entered his chambers.

There used to be a time when African Americans were called "Colored", but in looking at the different shades of purple and red running up and down Judge McCormick's normally pale white face, I began to question why that term wasn't given to Caucasian people instead. In his anger, his lily white face was extremely colored.

"You may all return to the courtroom. We will resume in ten minutes." Iron Hand Luke turned his back to us once again, and we took that as a signal to leave his chambers. We entered the courtroom one by one and as we came through the large swinging doors, the conversations in the room seem to change from loud clusters of noise to low consistent whispers. I felt all eyes on me and each glare seemed to pierce me with invisible knives.

As I walked to my steno machine, I passed Donald Murphy, the father of the victim who had sent the text message that ultimately resulted in the rescue of the girls. Mr. Murphy was a rather large man with a pot belly and an unrelenting air of intimidation around him. He had his arm around his wife's shoulder and if looks could kill, I would have dropped dead on the spot. I moved quickly to my machine and sat down. Seconds later the Bailiff announced that the judge was coming in.

"All rise. The Honorable Lucas McCormick presiding."

The low whispers turned to silence as the judge entered the courtroom. Iron Hand Luke took his seat and seemed to pause just long enough to make everyone in the room uncomfortable. It was clear to all that the action was done on purpose for added affect.

"Be seated. Ladies and Gentlemen

of the Jury, it is with extreme regret that I

must declare a mistrial in this case due to

procedural error. The counsels in this

case and you, yourselves, have done your

duty well concerning this trial, but due to

the error of the court reporter in this

proceeding, we do not have an accurate

record, and my hands are tied with

respect to my obligations for a fair trial. I

thank you for your time and for doing

your civic duty and you are released."

He slammed his gavel down and the Bailiff announced his exit.

"All Rise."

Lorraine Elzia

The level of noise in the courtroom rose again as the judge walked down from the bench toward his chambers once again. I began gathering my equipment and wanted nothing more than to disappear into the woodwork when I felt a tap on my shoulder.

"My daughter was raped once by Lionel Walker, and thanks to you, she has been raped again. With no lubrication or gentleness…thanks to you, she has been raped of her chance at vindication."

I was staring into the face of hate; the face of disgust; the face of Donald Murphy.

As long as I could remember, I had heard people outside of the judicial system state how corrupt the system was. Outsiders looking in always made comments that justice was never equal; money, social status and skin color dictated punishment received. At every instance and opportunity that I was confronted with statements of that nature, I felt an obligation to defend the complex nature of delivering justice and the beauty in making sure it was fair and impartial to all -- victims and defendants alike. The divinity of our legal system lay, at least in my mind, in protecting the rights of all parties. But as I looked in Mr. Murphy's face and his apparent hatred of me and a system that had failed him and his daughter, I cringed at the fact that the saying, "And Justice for All" really applied only if all conditions of the "fine print" were met. I was ashamed at myself for being the author of the tiny words at the bottom of Lionel's punishment contract which allowed sentencing for his crimes to become null and void.

Karma, It's a Mutha Fa Ya!

TGIF, Thank God It's Friday, never had more meaning than it did for me the day of the mistrial. I was banking on the probability that I wouldn't have to deal with Iron Hand Luke's punishment until Monday morning. After he declared a mistrial, I went to his chambers. He sat there with his reading glasses in his hand as he chewed on one of the handles, allowing the end of the glasses to dangle from his mouth. It was a habit of his which signified he was deep in thought. He looked at me sternly, straight in the eyes and said, "I'm very disappointed in you Kahla. I'm not sure what you are going through that would cause this much destruction in my court, but I am not in the right frame of mind to deal with you right now. I'm going to think about this over the weekend, clear my head and on Monday morning we will discuss your future, or lack thereof, as a Court Reporter in my court. You are dismissed."

Humbly, all I could say was, "Yes, Your Honor" as I left his chambers.

His delaying punishment on me was both a blessing and a curse. It was a blessing because I was too embarrassed and confused to defend my actions to him, so having a few extras days to pull myself together to come up with an excuse, was much needed. But it was a curse because if you ask any kid awaiting punishment from their parents, having to wait and see what is going to happen is much harder. You would find that most would much rather get the ass whooping over with, than to have to wait for days allowing their mind to torture itself contemplating what's going to happen.

I walked as quickly as I could to my office, trying to avoid seeing anyone and having to awkwardly act like everything was okay, when the exact opposite was true. As I opened the door to my office I stared at the diplomas on the wall and hysterically began to cry. I had held the tears in for so long, trying to be professional and strong, that my eyes exploded in grief once I was alone, safe behind the locked doors of my office. I looked at the thick mahogany, framed certificates on my recently painted plum colored walls, and felt as if everything I had worked so hard to accomplish would be taken away from me. Judge McCormick had the power to fire me and to recommend to the certification board that I lose my license. A reporter for the courts works at the pleasure of the judge; they can be fired at the will, with no explanations needed. But that was only one possibility; losing my job was one thing, losing my ability to continuing working in my field was another. My future, my career, and my lifestyle all rested in the judge's hands. My whole way of life was in jeopardy of being taken away from me because of my own actions or lack there of.

Why me?
Why this?
Why now?

The questions were flying at me and my emotions were overwhelming. It was one of those times in my life that I wished I smoked or did some sort of recreational drug so that I would have a way of releasing some of the tension I felt.

Mistress Memoirs

"I could sell my soul for a blunt right now." I made the proclamation loud and proud to myself; craving a way to escape to another place in my mind other than where I was.

I began pacing back and forth in my small, but quaint office. As I did, the room seemed to get smaller and smaller, almost suffocating me. My eyes shifted to the corner of the room and I saw my Crème-colored, *Dolce and Gabbana* Patent Leather shoulder bag resting on a stand. My tears stopped for a minute as I remembered the purse had been a gift from Kevin for Valentines Day. He had it wrapped in shiny red paper with a big white bow and brought it to me the night before Valentine's Day. I had showed it to him in a magazine about a week before telling him it was on my wish list of things to get for myself. I was pleasantly surprised to get it as a gift from him.

The card simply ready:
Fulfilling your desires, one wish at a time.
~Kevin

I wasn't even mad, at the time, at the fact that we had to celebrate the holiday the day before. I knew my place, I was number two, the runner up, so the real day had to be given to the winner, Valentine's Day had to sacredly be shared with his wife. I knew that; and acted accordingly at the time. I was just happy that he thought of me on the most romantic holiday of the year and bought me an expensive gift. That gesture was not lost on me, in spite of the circumstances.

Grabbing the purse, I hurriedly emptied its contents on my desk searching for a comfort I hoped laid therein. As my cell phone finally fell out I hit number one on the speed dial, calling the number one person in my life – Kevin. I got his answering machine --

Yo' dime; my time. Make em' both count.

I always hated that message; it irritated me since it reeked of arrogance. I refused to leave a message in response, and instead I only left my call back number.

I rubbed my freshly manicured hands across my blackberry anxiously and repeatedly, hoping against all

123

hope that if I rubbed it hard enough like *Aladdin* had, Kevin would appear just like the genie in the bottle did.

Home is my only sanctuary, I thought to myself. So I put all the beauty supplies of make-up, perfumes, and even my palm pilot and Altoids; along with all the other things that were thrown across the top of my desk; back in my purse and headed for the door and out of the courthouse. Luckily for me, everyone was long gone, either because of the mistrial or because it was lunchtime on a Friday afternoon. On the way to the parking lot, I hit redial. It had only been a few minutes since my last call to Kevin, but I prayed he would answer. I got his answering machine again. That time, I left a message.

"Call me Kevin. I need you."

As I said the words, I began to cry again.

I needed Kevin to soothe me. I needed *my man* to say, "Baby girl, it's going to be alright!" I was seeking *my man's* comfort even if he was a man I shared with another.

That day I had driven my favorite car -- a pearl colored Lexus SR 350 Roadstar convertible with the license plates, '4U2NV.' In comparison to my SUV, it was my sassy, little self-indulgence. I had paid for the car with cash made from the proceeds of a transcript of a very big case eight months prior. I chuckled to myself through my tears as I stared at it in the parking lot and thought, *No one envies me right about now, not even me.*

I turned on the engine and began driving, having no clue where I was going. It was eleven, forty five in the morning, just before noon and I just drove around letting Karma be my navigator and lead the way. The tears were flowing; I was on a course of self-hate and loathing when I noticed I was smack dab in the middle of down-town Chicago. I had been driving around in circles and was only a few blocks from where I started. – Still in walking distance of the courthouse. Amongst all the high-rise businesses and well-known bistros and restaurants stood a small, old cathedral; I'm not catholic, but something pulled me to the side of the road. Since I hadn't traveled far from where I started, I knew that roads couldn't take away my pain, but maybe divine intervention could. I parked on a meter, lay my head on the steering wheel, closed my eyes and asked God to just take me away.

"Fix my life Lord. Fix me now."

As I said the words I looked up and saw that the church bill board said there was a noon service. I took that as a sign I was supposed to go in.

Turning off the car, I slowly got out. I straightened my dress suit and thought to myself that I was presentable enough for church. I had toned down some of the sexiness of my outfits for the trial, so all areas that needed to be covered up; were. There were no tight skirts or busting tops since the trial had begun. I headed for the stairs of the church and as I got closer to the doors I looked up at the large cross on the top of the chapel. The rays of the sun were overpowering the sky behind the cross, casting a shadow down the stairs of the church which was mysterious yet heavenly; an omen of sorts.

"Give me a sign Lord; tell me what I am supposed to do with my life."

Be careful what you ask for.

As I thought the thought, I felt something on the side of my face. It was a feeling I hadn't felt before, but I knew it was the barrel of a gun. The cold metal against my temple, chilled both my thoughts and my footsteps in their paths. A gun has a way of commanding your attention pretty fast. I froze where I was and didn't say a word, but he did.

"How does it feel to be helpless Ms. Thompson? How does it feel to have your life in someone else's hands?" He pressed the revolver harder and harder into my temple. I winced in pain, then closed my eyes tightly as tears formed raindrops in the corners of my eyes, yet I didn't say a word.

Why couldn't the gun be in the hands of a mugger, someone that would take my purse and run; instead of in the hands of Donald Murphy, a man who thought, rightfully so, that I was the source of added pain to his family? At least with a mugger, I would have a chance. But there is no chance when the one on the other end of the gun has a personal vendetta against you.

I cringed further in fear as Mr. Murphy continued to speak.

"Are those tears Ms. Thompson? Are you crying? My daughter cried many a night. Do you know what stopped her tears? I'll tell you. It was the possibility of light at the end of a torturous tunnel. Her tears lessened when Lionel Walker was arrested. They were fewer in number when he was charged, and fewer still as the trial was in progress. She saw a light and her tears stopped with the thought that she was at the end of her personal nightmare. Then that light was put out. You helped it burn out, Ms. Thompson. Because of you, my daughter is crying again."

My lips quivered, snot rolled from my nose to my lips, but I was still able to control my mouth so that it remained silent. I controlled my mouth, yet I could not control my physical emotions. No matter how hard I squeezed my eyes shut, fear made the tears continue to fall in buckets with my nose running as well. My breathing was staggered and I made snorting noises as I saw my life flashing before my eyes. I felt like crying out for my mother, for a cop, for anyone or anything to save me. But I could sense that any utterance from me would agitate Mr. Murphy more. He was trigger happy and waiting for me to give him a reason, any excuse, to follow through with what he had came to do.

He moved closer to my face. His mouth, lips, and his breath were as close to my ears as the barrel of the revolver. The stench of his breath, a mixture of tobacco and coffee, made my skin crawl almost as much as his words when he whispered them in my ear, "I'll probably get the chair for this, but it will be worth it. I'll live out my last days knowing that you cried almost as much as my daughter did. For me, that will be enough. For me, my punishment for killing you will not be in vain. Karma is a mutha fa ya."

Karma. Is that what was at play in my life?

Karma? The thought got tossed around with

so many others swimming around in my

head. When you are faced with the possibility

Mistress Memoirs

of death, you can't control the order of the
scenes of the play, you just have to enjoy the
show and hope it all makes sense at the
intermission or when the fat lady sings.

As Donald Murphy said the words and I stiffened my body to prepare for the deadly shot I knew was about to come and splatter my brains along the streets of Chicago. As I thought about my parents and the pain they would suffer from hearing how I lost my life on the morning news, the bells of the cathedral rang.

It was high noon. -- The judgment hour; how ironic.

Twelve tolls of the bell rang out loudly for all within at least a mile's distance to hear. The ringing of the bells seemed heavenly; as if God were calling for a "time out" to all misconduct within ear's shot.

Donald Murphy seemed to be momentarily confused. He tilted his head sideways like a confused dog; studying me and studying the moment. Then he looked up at the sky, shook his head side to side and kind of chuckled in disbelief.

"Is that a sign Ms. Thompson? Is the ringing of the bells your salvation or your demise? Should your time be up, or do the bells ring to spare your life? Do the bells signify the beginning or the end? Tell me Ms. Thompson, what do you think the bells mean?"

He asked the questions, I gave no answers in response, just remained silent.

He caressed my face with the gun, running it slowly up and down the side of my jaw line in the same manner that one would caress the face of a lover with their hands.

He and I both contemplated his next move.

I opened my eyes as he placed the revolver to the tip of my nose.

"For whom does the bell toll Ms. Thompson? ANSWER ME!"

I looked him straight in the eye, whimpered and said, "It tolls for me."

Sloppy Seconds

Donald Murphy had made his statement. Making me piss in my pants was all he had really come to do that day. -- He achieved his goal.

After I uttered the words of the *final bell tolling for me*, Donald smiled, hit me up side my head lightly with the gun in the same manner a mother would hit a defiant child, and then he said, "Both you and I know what time it was Ms. Thompson. Don't you ever forget how differently this could have ended; because I never will." He chastised me with his eyes and his words. And although he appeared quickly, he disappeared slowly and gradually, allowing the moment to linger.

Even though Donald felt the need to give me the strong reprimand of how my continued existence was "allowed" by him, the reprimand wasn't needed. Who could ever almost lose their life and then just forget about it? I knew I never would.

I watched him walk off, leaving me soiled and scared; but alive. When he was at a distance that I knew I could out run him if he chose to come back and finish what he started, I fell to my knees and kissed the sidewalk with both my lips and my soul. For a summer's day in

Chicago, the concrete was amazingly cool, gelid to my cheeks as I lay with my face on the pavement. I guess living in the windy city has its advantages when you are face down on a sidewalk needing a cool breeze to lower your anxieties and blood pressure at the same time.

Never in my life had the dirty sidewalks of Chicago seemed so comforting to my entire being. I did not care who saw me. I did not care about the dirt on my expensive suit or what I looked like. I did not care if my makeup was running from crying or if my hair was a mess, or who saw me kissing the curb. I was just happy to be alive and recognized that I had been given a second chance at life. I didn't know why I had been spared, but I was thankful for it. Mr. Murphy held the option of erasing me from the face of the earth, and yet he walked away, allowing me to live. His mercy on me during a moment that told him to be merciless is something that would remain with me until the day I ceased to be on this side of the dirt.

While on my knees, hugging the payment, like someone with a hangover hugs a toilet bowl, I was thankful for my life being spared and I regurgitated all my sins and acknowledged my thankfulness through prayer.

When I was done, I pulled myself together and moved to a bench under a tree and called Kevin. As much as I needed a change of clothes, I needed solace more. I had been through hell and back on the steps of a church and needed the comfort I thought only he could give me. My day started out bad and just continued to go down with each passing hour to say the least, and I needed *my man* to make reality go away and replace it with tranquility. I couldn't push speed dial fast enough.

The line rang three times before he answered.

"Thank God, I finally can talk to you." I blurted out once I heard his voice on the other end of the line.

I began speaking fast, exhilarated at the fact that he had answered and seeking comfort I thought only he could give me.

"Kevin, you will not believe all the shit that happened to me today. I need to talk to you. I need to get all of this out of my head before I explode. Can you meet me at home?" My words were deliberate in delivery. Only a fool would not have noticed my desperation.

Whispers controlled his response. His words were barely audible. I imagined him hiding in a corner with his hands cupped around the receiver so I could hear him. He sounded agitated.

"Kahla, I can't talk right now. You know what weekend this is. We talked about it for weeks. I am in the Pocono's. It's Nicole's birthday. Can you call me on Sunday? We'll be back in a couple of days, and I *probably* can sneak away then for a little while to meet you. Just give me till then baby girl, but I can't possibly talk to you now, Kahla. She's at the bar right now, so I have a moment, but come on girl, can't this wait till Sunday?"

His response was self absorbed, incognizant of my needs. It was a *"me, me, me,"* world for Kevin; he hadn't heard a word I said.

Sunday?

Poconos?

Nichole's Birthday?

What the hell? Was that nigger serious?

My life had been shaken, not stirred, poured out to me straight on the rocks with no chaser; and all *my man* could offer to me in the way of condolences was that he was in the Poconos with his freakin' wife while I was sitting under a tree in wet underwear!

All hell to the nawh! I thought. It was clear to me that he was just a squirrel trying to get a nut. And I was definitely a nut for ever allowing him to enter my heart.

This can't possibly be happening; especially when dealing with his ass was what had landed me in all the positions concerning my life that I found myself in.

I visualized pages on a calendar with the months slowly falling off, one by one, and I began to total up how much time, effort and energy I had given to Kevin. Months of my life had been stolen, they were gone and I would never be able to get them back.

It was August, the eight month of the calendar year; the fifth month of the zodiac; the reign of Leo the lion.

Nicole was a Leo.

Lorraine Elzia

I should have known it before that moment. While not a true follower of the Zodiac signs and horoscope, I did believe that the moon controlled birth and that people born under certain signs did posses the same qualities and traits.

How befitting of Nicole to be the lioness, wearing the crown of the most pompous, patronizing, bossy and full of themselves sign of the zodiac.

Yet he was with her instead of me.

No matter how much mud I wanted to sling, or how many daggers I wanted to throw at the arrogance of Leos, and the fact that Nicole was a tried and true Leo in every shape, form and fashion of the sign; the fact still remained that he was with her instead of the loving arms of the Cancer he had on the side.

He was at a bar with his wife, the Leo, in the Poconos; while whispering excuses into the ears of his Cancer Mistress on the phone.

That was the case at hand; that was reality.

He chose her over me. My moment was insignificant and hers was monumental enough to warrant a trip to the Poconos.

He was spending quality time with her, while rushing me off the phone with promises of "probably" seeing me on Sunday when he could "sneak" away. I was nothing more than his dirty little secret and I regretted signing up for the role.

My drama was coincidental to his plans, an irritance of sorts to him, but important enough to me for me to re-evaluate "our thang." I'm sure Kevin had no idea of the importance of the call and his failure to act. I am sure he did not know that the phone call was one of those moments of a line drawn in the sand. Moments that change situations for one person, while the other stands clueless.

Right then, for me, a line was drawn, Kevin crossed it, and a tide came and erased it away as if it never existed. But in my mind it did. At that moment, as insignificant as the phone call was…things were defined for me. Things that I did not want to open my eyes to before.

Mistress Memoirs

I began to feel dirty. Muddy on the inside and out in all aspects that concerned Kevin and my involvement with him. I desired a shower; wanting to see all ruminants of him and our affair to go down the drain. My feelings of love for Kevin had been contaminated by the repugnant fact that I would always be the runner up; never the winner. Nicole took first place, and no matter what I did when it came to him, it was clear that I would always be inferior to his loyalty to her, no matter how many *sweet nothings* he whispered in my ear after sex to the contrary, my ranking was apparent and written on the wall for all to see.

Actions speak louder than words.

He could shout his undying love for me, but his actions spoke a deeper love for his wife.

When it came to Kevin's love and how he dished it out…he served mine in a whisper and hers with a scream.

I would always be apple pie, while she would always be pie with a scoop of ice cream on top.

She would always be the *a'la mode* to my existence in his life.

At that moment, it was as if someone had put smelling salt under my nose to trigger my ability to inhale the truth of the situation and exhale the fiction. Although I had thought it before, it never sunk in until that phone call. When it came to my relationship with Kevin in comparison to his relationship with his wife; sloppy second was all I was, and sloppy second was all I would ever be.

Diamond Dust

You have bamboozled my mind
Transparent
And free from flaws.

My thoughts adore you
Worshipping the ground you walk on
dreaming of drinking your bath water
until I am inebriated with you at all costs.

Then a brick fell on my head
The picture shattered
Awakening my senses to reality

Rose colored glasses removed
Picture clearer
I'm now in a more stable mentality.

You're not a diamond,
As I thought,
dear lover of my soul

You're more like
Diamond dust.
Not even glittering
like pure gold.

You're not rainbows
Or sunshine
Nor anything composed
along loving lines

You're nothing more
than precipitation
on my otherwise
warm and sunny sky.

You put on a mask
That I accepted

Lorraine Elzia

But as of today
Your fakeness
no longer flies

Where I thought
there was perfection
I now realize
does not reside

My bad....
dear loved one,
I shouldn't have
lifted you up so high

I put you in a place
and a position where
You could never
holistically abide

For perfection
you are not.
In you
perfection
is just a blur.

The problem lies,
Not in whom
you presented to me
But in whom
I assumed you were

The pedestal
I put you on crumbles
The expectation....
at minimum is
downsized.

A Diamond
you were to me
But now
you are merely

Mistress Memoirs

diamond dust
In my eyes.

Kahla

The Me Factor

I cracked the seal on a bottle of Monnet VSOP Cognac. It was a housewarming gift from a coworker who, in buying it, showed that they apparently didn't know me all that well. But, a gift is a gift, and who was I to look an expensive gift horse in the mouth. So I accepted it and placed it in the mini bar in my family room. I had already received two very large Cognac glasses reminiscent of Al Pacino's character in *Scarface*, so I used the trademark glasses to flank the bottle on both sides. Since I hadn't been a drinker since college, I had lost my taste for liquor and the bottle hadn't been open in the seven years that had expired since I bought my house.—But it sure looked cute and sophisticated on my bar.

The seal was cracked because I needed a narcotic high that day. I hoped the brandy would do the trick. As I watched the flow of the aged-to-perfection liquid fill the large, monogram-engraved, *Ridell* crystal, I cradled the cognac glass between my ring and middle fingers swirling it around like I had seen in Al's movie and I sniffed the fragrance of anticipated intoxication. Taking a sip, I felt the warmth of the swallow, and began asking myself the questions that were ballooning in my mind.

Did he love me?

Was it all just a game?

As more swallows of Cognac followed, my mind went around in circles trying to figure out the answers.-- Rewinding conversations, memories and situations in my head trying to decipher them like Morris Code. I thought that knowing the real answers to the questions of his love and the status of our relationship, was what I needed.

Then it hit me.

I wouldn't ever really and truly know those answers, and in actuality, the answers to those questions were irrelevant.

Even if he didn't love me and was just playing a mind game with me, that wouldn't erase our history; it wouldn't change our past.

His part in our screen play was his and his alone. There was no need for auditions; the part was already taken.

Those were his feelings. His emotions.

I didn't own them, neither did anyone else; he did. I had to come to grips with that and with the fact that for me, what was more important was my ability to diagnose what made me fall into the affair in the first place. That's what I really needed to seek an answer to.

Mirror, mirror on the wall, why did I become his mistress after all?

Everything else was irrelevant, and that was the million-dollar question. The one that needed to be answered.

Did I take on the role because I was lonely? Yeah, that was part of it.

Did I become a willing partner to the affair because my biological clock was ticking? -- Possibly and more than likely, probably.

I weighed all the supporting crutches to my injured behavior and ultimately had to reconcile that despite the fact that my "fronts" were up to the contrary; it all boiled down to my self-esteem--a feeling of discontent within me. All of the events concerning Kevin came about because of how I categorized and viewed myself.

I allowed myself to be used goods because I needed someone else to complete and make me whole.

What a sad revelation; but an enlightening one as well.

While successful in my own right, there was still a void in my existence, a black hole that needed to be filled. I came to terms with the fact that I was not truly comfortable enough in my own skin and was looking for a tailor; someone to alter my life in a manner that made it cling to me ever-so-perfectly and presentably in the sight of others. Kevin seemed to fit my altercation needs.

Sometimes a girl can fool herself, or best case scenario, at least try.

In the pursuit of being Barbie, we obtain Barbie's dream house, her convertible, and her clothes all the while telling ourselves that when we get Ken, then and only then, will we be complete. Every fairy tale ends with the prince and the princess living happily ever after. We learn that even before kindergarten. All great love stories end with the two characters becoming one. Everything we see, read and hear tells us that much. Our media and our history promoted the union of a man and woman. Being single does not fit into what we view as being successful, or as being happy. I bought into the commercialized view of what a real woman was, and what accessories she *needed* to have in order to be happy; to be complete.

We all have feelings associated with our own self-worth; dreams which are fostered in us as a child of who we will be when we grow up. Even fairy tales tell us, "Give me my prince and then I am complete…then I am worthy!"

Expectations can be a self-fulfilling prophesy.

As such we jump through the hoops to achieve the goals. We think that life is a manufactured puzzle where all the pieces will ultimately fit together "perfectly" if we just have the patience to take the time and place each piece, ever so carefully where it belongs. Reality is that sometimes the pieces don't fit; sometimes we try to force a round piece into a square shaped spot.

My life was a puzzle.

All the pieces were in place except the last one...the vital puzzle piece of companionship. The piece that would allow me to scream out to the rest of the world in victory, "LOOK AT ME, FINALLY I'M DONE; I'M COMPLETE."

Maybe I had grown tired of patiently putting the pieces together and that's why I forced an unfitting piece into a position in which it did not belong. I wanted so badly for the puzzle of my life to be complete, that I forgot the adage of "if it don't fit, don't force it."

Kevin didn't fit, but I was forcing it.

Why?

Probably, because I had grown tired of trying to put the pieces of the puzzle together. The game was getting old and my patience was growing thin. I wanted to master the puzzle *by any means necessary.* I wanted the final product to be done so I could move on to the next project. I needed that closure. That's why Kevin got in. I was tired of moving around pieces that "almost fit."

He may have used me, whether intentional or not, but I allowed his "renting" of my love because I was weak and needed a buyer, or at the very least, someone willing to take out a long-term lease.

Wrong person; right time.

That was the extent of our relationship. I had blossomed and bloomed on the vine of life and was ripe for the picking. The problem was that the wrong farmer came along to harvest the crop.

Kevin strolled in--no, I take that back, it was more like a swagger--when I was smack dab in the middle of a vortex of need; a whirlpool of trying to make any warm body help me feel complete. Someone of substance that I could pour into my ready-made mold. Unbeknownst to me at the time, I was defunct of rational thinking when I allowed him into my life. I thought I was in love, but as an old song says, *It takes a fool to learn that love don't love nobody.* If I were in my right mind, from the moment I searched for love in Kevin, I would have searched instead

Mistress Memoirs

for love within myself. The spotlight in my lighthouse would have shined brightly upon me, instead of searching for a ship passing in the night. I would have searched for ways to be happy being alone; content within myself, satisfied within just me.

After the fact, I realized that I was in pain; enormous and overwhelming pain. And when you are hurting, you just want the pain to go away the quickest way possible.

You don't really appreciate and recognize that sometimes when it comes to pain; you can't go around it; you have to go through it.

Instead of pinpointing my own self-esteem issues and going "through" the process of healing them; I chose to try and go "around" them instead by having the affair.

I sat weighing my actions and realized that I wasn't *okay* being alone, and the fact that I wasn't able to be alone should have been a red flag to me. Because if I couldn't be *okay* being alone, and couldn't be *okay* with just being me, how could I ever be *okay* being with someone else?

I sat back in my chaise lounge, took another sip of cognac and marinated on the "Wow" moment I was having.

I began to accept the fact that Kevin had gotten in because I had felt a strange feeling of entitlement to a man and a "respectable" way of life.

In feeling that way, somewhere along the road, things got twisted, I missed the mark and I allowed myself to snatch someone else's man, and their respectable way of life.—Pretending it was my own. In wanting to complete who I was, I had become satisfied in borrowing someone else's puzzle piece to help complete the enigma of me.   I had allowed the inclusion of a man, in my life or lack thereof, to define me. Being single had become a scarlet letter to me; a mark that allowed others to judge who I was and the quality of my life. It was an ear mark of my ranking in society; or so I thought. And just like Nathaniel Hawthorne's 1850's character Hester Prynne, I struggled to escape the public shame of the scarlet letter displayed prominently on my bossom and my entire being. My singleness seemed to define me as if I had been branded for all to see. I was second class or at least "B" list to my married counterparts. I wanted desperately to move pass my scarlet letter tattoo and I tried to create a life of dignity and social acceptance while wearing my badge of shame.

The fact that I was not a part of a Mr. and Mrs. and did not carry a man's last name as my own had become distasteful to the palate of my own self image.

When I evaluated my self worth, I was embarrassed that even with my attainment of certain wealths in life; I was poor and lacking when measured by what was truly a sign of having *arrived* in life. That "arrival" as defined by society, was limited by the parameters of the inclusion of a man in a woman's life. Being connected to a man by a matrimonial umbilical cord symbolized success; anything less meant you "hadn't quite made it." Without the title of Mrs. So and So, you could cross the finish line, but you don't win the prize. Stupidly, I bought into that definition.

Anxiety over being single was knocking at my door; I shouldn't have answered when the bell rang; or if I did answer, I should have redirected the visitor to the door steps of another house on the block.

But I didn't.

I answered the knock of "single anxiety" and welcomed in the demon of temptation and the spirit of envy, who quickly took the helm in the cockpit of my love life. My low self esteem allowed me to move from a position of self containment and self sufficiency to a position of dependence on the existence of a man in my world.

Was Kevin the culprit of my self-transformation?

No. He was not the guilty party, but he was a tool.

As much as I would have liked to join the ranks of women who place blame of their actions in life on some slimy, no-good man; I couldn't do that. For me, there could be no excuses; no shifting of blame.

Just like Kevin had to *own* his feelings and his participation in *our* thang; I had to do the same thing as well. It takes two to tango. Kevin had not dragged and abducted me in the darkness of night, handcuffed, kicking and screaming into an adulterous affair. I went along willingly, almost subserviently, as if in a cult-like mentality to everything he suggested; everything he proposed and planned.

Our thang was consensual.

I was just as guilty, if not more, in the part I played in the affair.

He had his reasons for wanting "a piece on the side," doesn't every adulterer; male or female alike?

He was the one that took the marital vows and had to atone for breaking them. But I wasn't innocent in *our* sin. I was not a prisoner in our transgression. I had to take responsibility for my willing patronage of being his mistress. He may have placed a piece of gourmet cheese on a string over my head to tempt me, but I had to own up to the fact that I was still the rat that chased the cheese at all cost.

So just like any rat whose tail is caught in a trap, I had to accept the fact that I was still the one that followed the temptation and took the bait.

What does his waiving cheese over my head say about Kevin? A whole lot. He had some logs in the *affair* fire as well. He will have to deal with the fact that he ignited the fire for the rest of his life, and he will have to answer to his maker about that. That's between him and his creator. But I contributed to the embers of the fire as well. My low self esteem was the match that allowed everything else to be set a blaze. As much as I hated to admit it, I was the essential ingredient that allowed every other motion to be set in play.

Why hadn't I been content with being alone until I was blessed with the mate God had chosen for me?

Why couldn't I resist temptation when placed in my face?

Why hadn't I been able to utter the words that the famous first lady, Nancy Regan told the nation two decades earlier of "Just Say No?"

Why hadn't all the things I had been told growing up about respecting myself too much to let any man or anything else interrupt my path to greatness?

What had made the shadier side of life more alluring to me than what I knew in my heart to be the yellow brick road to meeting my goals?

The answer to all of that lay simple in the word, "Me."

I was my roadblock.

I was my distraction.

My low self esteem was the tool.

Self gratification was the goal.--Bottom line.

The ultimate culprit to my demise was me, and only me. None of the things that were ruining my life would have been able to set up roots, blossom or grow without the *Me* factor.

As hard as it was for me to admit the error of my ways, or more importantly the reasons for the mistake in the first place…everything that took me to the land of the other woman had been facilitated, not by a man with smooth lines, a tight body and a million dollar smile; but my road to destruction was paved with the stones of my own insecurities, bordered all along the way with flowers of self hate, which were watered by a need to be presentable in the eyes of others.

I alone was the seed, fertilizer and water that allowed the affair to be nurtured and to grow.

I was the inner gun that shot a bullet at my outward being.

I was the one that hung a noose around my own head and committed suicide upon who I was and the direction of my life.

I was the one that allowed criticism of who I was, to slowly chip away at what I was building myself up to be.

Everything that went "immoral" in my life, boiled down to the factor of ME.

There are only speed bumps in life.

There are no stop signs unless they are self imposed.

No one can make us *Stop*, or for that matter, *Go* forward in life, but for our own willingness to put the pedal to the metal and move.

As much as I would have loved to place the blame squarely on his shoulders, Kevin did not drive the car that took me to the land of being a mistress. He was the gas, but ultimately, I was the vehicle itself; me and my low self esteem. While neither can function without the other; a vehicle plays a much more prominent part in traveling than gas does.

I had often wondered why wives, who found out their husbands were cheating on them, would take their anger out on the girlfriend. When speaking to my friends in the past about the subject, as I spoke in my holier than thou voice, I would tell them that any woman who caught her man cheating needed to deal with that man, placing the blame where it belonged and leave the girlfriend alone. My advice was that instead of taking off shoes, removing earrings and rubbing Vaseline on their face to get ready to kick his *girl on the side's* ass; they should take out their anger on their husband, the one that had truly betrayed them. My thoughts in the past had always been that the girlfriend was not the one that had committed a crime; the lying, cheating husband had.

But standing on the other side of the equation; being a partner to the crime of the affair, and objectively categorizing my participation, my thoughts had changed. As the mistress, I was guiltier than the husband. I was guilty because I allowed myself to be used. I allowed myself to violate someone else's marriage because of my selfish wants and my needs.

Yeah, maybe he would have done it anyway, if not with me, with someone else. But if each woman that decided to spread her legs and allow a married man to enter therein, would stop in her tracks and ask herself why she is in that position, and then exam what's going on in her own head that allowed her to find sharing another woman's man to be an attractive idea--then maybe, just maybe, "that" affair wouldn't happen. If each potential mistress would push 'pause' on her actions long enough to take a look at herself, her frame of mind, and the 'why' of what she is contemplating before engaging in the relationship, there would be less affairs committed.

In the scheme of the road to an affair, I was much more of a guilty party than Kevin was. In analyzing how we both got "caught up," I played a larger role. When weighing the factors that brought about the entire situation of *me and he*...the ingredient that allowed the affair to happen was my low self esteem. The yeast that allowed the affair to rise was ME.

Screeching Halt

The Sabbath Day announced its arrival with a call on my cell phone at eight, forty five a.m. I was startled and awakened from my drunken slumber by the sound of the music of my ring tone coupled with my cognac glass hitting the hard-wood floor beneath me. Intoxicated by both the Brandy and my thoughts, I had passed out the night before in my chaise lounge in the living room trying to avoid reality.

I rubbed the crusted aftermath of sleep from my eyes, and looked in the direction of my *Casa Cristina* end table as my cell phone blared Sean Kingston's "Beautiful Girls" at the highest volume possible over and over again like an old 45 record that was scratched.

Inebriated beyond any measurable point I had been in my life, I fumbled with the buttons to try and answer the call, but my actions were slow in motion and I took too long to answer, so the call went to my voice mail. I stared at the neon message of a missed call and was only able to think to myself that whoever it was would have to hear from me later, because I had cotton mouth that was out of this world and wouldn't be able to talk coherently if I tried. I rolled over recognizing that my telephone butler would take care of my phone guest.

As I lavished in the comfort of the space of the chaise lounge and cursed the sun's rays which were beating upon me and my hangover, I felt a gnawing feeling to throw up. My whole body was on fire from the inside and I could feel the alcoholic contents of my stomach traveling the long journey up to my mouth. I was instantaneously reminded that I couldn't hold my liquor as I once did when I was younger and in college. I raced to the porcelain God housed in the guest bath on the first floor. As I glanced at the pristine towels that collected dust on the towel rack because they were merely a form of decoration and not for actual use, I grabbed one on my way to the floor as I began to feel liberated as the sins of the night before purged themselves from my body.

A veteran drinker knows that Cognac is smooth going down, but kicks ass when coming back up. I wasn't a veteran, and the term novice was even strong when it came to describing me and my adult drinking skills.

Cuddling the toilet, I felt like a criminal who got caught during the commission of his first crime, who wished he had got busted when he was more skilled in the game and had at least reaped some of the benefits of committing the crime.

But alcohol poisoning doesn't take a resume of its potential candidates, it treats all applicants the same, and I was paying the price for the drinking crime of the night before. I released the demons of the previous night until I could no longer give up the liquid ghost. Once I got to the point of dry heaving, I decided to put something solid in my stomach to try and absorb the monkey that was on my back.

I went to the kitchen, turned on the mounted counter-top TV, and prepared to make breakfast. I pulled the eggs from the refrigerator and grabbed the bread from the second shelf, deciding that some dry toast was in order as well. I placed the eggs on the griddle, put my cell phone on its holder and pushed the button to activate the speaker phone.

"Please enter your password" I heard the mechanical voice say.

I entered ten ten; Kevin's birthday.

"You have one new message. To listen to your messages press one."

I obliged and as the recorded phone message began, I flipped to WGN on the TV to catch the local morning news show that I rarely got a chance to see, and I began to scramble the eggs.

Brian's voice on my machine sounded shaky. I tried to focus and concentrate on what he was saying, but my brain was liquid mush, and tuned in instead to the flashing bright colors of the bulletin at the top of the TV screen which interrupted the program with a blond anchor woman sporting over-bleached hair and too much make up.

"This just in; we are taking you live to the

scene of a hostage situation at the Field

Museum on Lake Shore Drive. The museum

which is located close to Soldier's Field,

has been a local source of entertainment,

discovery, learning and excitement to

school-age children and citizens alike since

1921. Today it is the scene of death, horror

and fear.

The anchor woman's voice was dramatic, yet you could tell she was reading from a teleprompter. As I listened to her, an eerie sensation surrounded me. I cupped my hands under the faucet in the kitchen sink, ran the water and splashed the filtered substance on my face to try and lessen the effects of my hangover. I dried my face with a paper towel and I barely heard the beep that signaled the end of Brian's message. I had no clue what he said, but I instinctively turned up the volume on the TV and gave the obviously inexperienced anchor woman my full attention, even though her incompetence irritated me.

Lorraine Elzia

"Three armed gunman entered the museum today in an attempt to take a share of the morning's ticket sales. Chicago police were called to the scene when a cashier pressed the silent alarm button while cooperating with the gunmen's requests that she turn over the money she collected. The police arrived within minutes of the distress call and entered the museum. The gunman began open fire on the police; killing three, wounding two others, and holding the cashier and several tour guides hostage. The names of the officers wounded and killed in the line of duty are being withheld at this time and hostage negotiators have been called to the scene. We will update you on this breaking story as it develops."

The channel went back to the regularly scheduled morning show which was in the middle of demonstrating how to make some low-fat breakfast shake which was the newest diet craze.

Side note: Fad Diets; been there, done that, just under a different celebrity name.

"Wow" I thought. "This city gets more dangerous with each passing day. Its sad kids can't even go to the museum without crime rearing its ugly head. That's just senseless madness. What's the world coming to?"

I tuned out the morning violence, and put two pieces of wheat grain bread in the toaster. I put salt and pepper on my eggs as I started my phone messages over from the beginning.

Ten ten was entered once again. The significance of the password to the message wasn't apparent at the time.

Brian's voice began again; still solemn in tone and nature.

"Kahla, when you get this message call me. Better yet, go to Cedar Memorial Hospital. Kevin was shot this morning and he is asking for you. He told his doctor to tell me to call you. I don't have any more details, that's all I know. Even though I don't condone your relationship with him, I'm honoring his request by calling you. He wants to see you, so get there as soon as you can."

A dial tone ended the message.

My eyes widened, and in a moment I was stone-cold sober. Coffee has nothing on the sobering effect of a call of distress. I removed my cell phone from its perch and pressed Brian's number, praying he was still available to talk. He answered after the fourth ring.

"This is Brian."

"Brian, I just got your message. Tell me this is some sick joke. Is Kevin really in the hospital? What happened? Is he alright?

Unlike my conversation with Brian before Kevin and I got "involved", where I was able to portray a non-chalant attitude concerning Kevin, this time my voice signaled my affection and concern.

"Kahla, he was answering the call for assistance over at the museum this morning and got shot three times while trying to enter the building. He's alive and in ICU, but that's all I know. Go to him Kahla, he's asking for you."

The desperation in Brian's voice said it all. I responded with four simple words before hanging up –
"I'm on my way."

The moments following the call are all a blur to me. I vaguely remember turning off the food that was cooking, running upstairs, throwing on a jogging suit, grabbing my keys and driving the fifteen miles to Cedar Memorial. I don't know what thoughts ran through my mind other than needing to be by Kevin's side.

The hospital was close to the museum. Kevin was probably taken there because it was the only hospital within thirty miles of where he had been shot. As I walked to the entrance of the hospital, the doors automatically separated and upon entering I immediately thought I was in a war zone. The Emergency Room reeked of sickness, death and disease. Every seat was taken and there were patients in wheel chairs while others lay out with blankets on the floor. Most of the people in the waiting room looked like they had already been medicated in an effort to help weather the long wait before they could actually see a doctor; while others looked like drug addicts there in the hopes of scoring some methadone to fight the symptoms of withdrawal.

I walked passed the medical zombies to the receptionist desk.

"Can you tell me how to get to ICU?"

The nurse was chewing on her gum like a cow chews cud. She raised her eyes up in my direction and began patting the top of her head like women do when their weave is too tight or itching and they don't want to disrupt the spots that adhere the tracks to their head. She had more concern for her $36.00, eighteen inch, 1B# human hair extensions, than she had about my need to find a love one admitted in the hospital. She wore large hoop earrings with the word "Baby Phat" in cursive writing in the middle.

"Yeah Baby, you FAT all right!" I said to myself as I watched her squirm her large frame in her chair trying to get more comfortable.

She responded, "Who you here fo'?" Her ebonic question and attitude were working my last nerve.

"I'm here to see Kevin Eckhart; he was one of the officers brought in from the museum shooting today. How do I get to ICU?" My irritation level was rising and you could hear it in my words.

"You family? How I know you ain't with the news or somethin'? You related to him? Only family can get in there. It's my ass if I let you up there and you ain't family." The hood rat nurse gave me much attitude as she said the words, while rolling her head as if a screw was loose that normally held it in place.

I rolled my eyes at her and then I had to check myself. Nurse Ghetto was right. I WASN'T family. Quiet as kept, to the world I was nothing of importance to him at all. I had no right to information about him or to anything about him at all.

I didn't give her question or her ghetto attitude the dignity of a response. I turned and walked through the graveyard of a waiting room and began to sulk on my way to the front door.

"Who do you think you are Kahla? The man is in ICU. He needs his family right now, not his booty call with benefits. Know your place girl and stay in it." My mind began to chastise me. I asked myself what right DID I have to be in the hospital ranting and raving about wanting to see MY man; a man that was mine only as a time share at best.

Feeling remorseful that I had even come to the hospital in the first place, I continued walking out the door and toward my car. Then just as quickly as the thoughts that I did not belong there had pushed its way into my head; my heart began to fight back screaming of entitlement.

Even if I was sharing a man, that meant he was at least "half" mine. With all that Kevin and I had shared together, I was "entitled" to at least see him.

Maybe I wasn't "family" in the traditional sense of the word, but I did have a place in his life, and he in mine.

I turned around and went back through the automatic doors, passed the walking-dead patients, passed the gloom and doom of the waiting area to my final destination of the information board. There's more than one way to skin a cat. Head Ghetto Nurse might not have given me the info I needed, but that didn't mean I wasn't going to get it.

I ran my eyes over the board that dictated the location of each section of the hospital and as I glanced at the data for each of the floors listed, I saw that the ICU unit was on the seventh floor.

"Bingo!" I screamed within.

I got on the elevator not knowing what I would do when the doors opened. The elevator parted on the seventh floor to glass-encased rooms. I could see a receptionist desk down the hall to the left, so I instinctively went to the right to avoid detection. There were about seven rooms on that side of the floor.

"Father, please let him be on this side. Let me see him, without having to cause any drama." I hoped God was hearing my sincere prayer.

As I walked passed the first two rooms and noticed human-like entities lying in beds looking anything but humanly, I took in the vision that each room was wide open and the life containment machines and Iv's were visible to all prying eyes. My heart dropped at the sorrow that engulfed that portion of the hospital. The constant beep of heart monitors could be heard outside each room. Some sounding steady, having hope; others sounding weak and irregular with anticipation that they would stop at any minute. Decomposition of life permeated the entire floor. I continued walking past the tiny rooms and looked ahead only long enough to see Nichole walking towards me under the arm of a doctor. I moved closer to the room I was in front of and stood outside of it pretending I was staring at the lifeless body that lay therein and lowering my head as if deep in prayer. As Nichole and the doctor passed me, I heard their conversation. Nichole was crying hysterically and the doctor was trying to comfort her.

"Mrs. Eckhart, we just are unsure of the exact damage done to his heart and lungs. At least you were able to talk to him right now. I don't know how long he will be coherent like he is, so take some comfort that you were able to tell him before he went into surgery that you loved him and that he was able to hear and understand you. We are doing all we can, but I need to be

honest with you and say that the next few hours
are crucial and mean life or death for your
husband. Go get some coffee. In a few minutes he
will be wheeled into the operating room and we
will remove the bullets. We have a small chapel
on the first floor. If you are a religious woman
go there now and pray for the life of your
husband. He's been given a sedative and will be
out of it shortly, he won't feel any pain. I will do
my best, but my hands are only human; put your
trust not in my hands, but in the hands of God."

They both walked passed me, oblivious to my existence, just like Nichole had been for my entire affair with Kevin. Unaware that I was ever in the vicinity, let alone in her backyard.

As they got farther and farther away from me, I seized the moment and continued walking in the direction from which they had come from. After passing two more rooms, I saw him.

I stopped mid step.

A nurse was standing over him writing on a clip board. My first sight of the man I loved was one of bereavement. He looked like an octopus with all the extensions of tubes coming out of every orifice of his body and some new holes that intravenous needles had created. He was breathing through a cup over his mouth that looked like a jock strap. I could sense and see his pain. He looked weak and helpless. The virile man I had known and loved was not the same one that lay in that bed. The man in that bed was fragile and weak, hanging on to life by the skin on his pearly white teeth. The sight of him in that condition took me to a place of mental mourning.

"Mr. Eckhart, can you hear me? We will be taking you to surgery in a few minutes. I have given you a pretty strong anesthesia. As soon as it takes full effect I will take you to the operating room. You're going to be all right. Don't worry about anything. You are in good hands."

Even from the other side of the glass window, I didn't believe her, so I knew Kevin didn't either.

I wanted to walk in the room, grab him and tell him how much he meant to me. But my feet were frozen in place. I knew the nurse would never let me in the room, so I had to be content looking at him from afar. I owed him the respect of not making a scene.

"Stay in your place Kahla." I sternly reminded myself.

I saw him smile at his nurse and weakly give her the thumbs up sign. I felt a sensation of extreme pride. Kind of like when you witness a heroic moment. He was a true trooper in every situation. Brave even when his heart told him not to be. I was proud that I had let him in my life.

And then he looked in my direction. Our eyes connected and mine widened in width as I instinctively knew he "felt" my presence and we were one again for the moment. I could tell his body was letting go due to the anesthesia, but his heart was trying to hold on to me. I placed my face as close to the glass barrier that separated his world at that minute from mine, and I put my entire hand up to the glass to show him that I wanted to be with him. He coughed briefly, and as the nurse bent over to readjust the tubes sticking out of his mouth, he looked me directly in the eye and raised his finger; with it he pointed to his eye, and then drew an outline in the air of a heart, then he pointed to me.

I – heart- you.

I ran his charade message through my brain, hung my head and began to silently cry. I placed both of my hands over my heart, hoping to capture the moment in my body forever.

He was saying, "I love you."

I returned the same message, using my finger to point to my eye, then outlining a heart in the air, pointed at him, followed by two fingers.

My message to him: "I love you too."

Our means of communication seemed to have drained Kevin. After he saw my reply, he laid his slightly elevated torso back on the bed and I heard the heart machine go dead.

FLAT LINE!!

I had seen enough movies to know what that meant and what would come next.

"Cold Blue, Code Blue." The nurse was screaming at the top of her lungs, pushing all kinds of buttons, and people in white lab coats and scrubs came rushing from all corners of the floor towards my direction.

No one questioned me. They didn't have time for that, they just said, "We're going to have to ask you to leave ma'am."

"Ma'am?"

"Ma'am!" I always hated that word in certain context. To me it was a polite way of saying, "Bitch."

It was condescending.

I wished I could tell them ALL that I wasn't just a "Ma'am." I WAS somebody in his life. He just had told me as much. Maybe I wasn't Wifey...but I was more than just a Ma'am. If they wanted to give me a title as they were trying to save my man's life...call me his Mistress. Call me his woman. Call me his love...that's what HE called ME.

As the hospital personnel pulled out machines to electronically shock Kevin's heart, I didn't want to be dismissed. I wanted recognition of "our" thang. I wanted everyone to know that the man on the table WAS mine. He had answered all my questions of the night before with a few gestures delivered by his weak and fragile fingertips.

As Kevin's body continued to Flat line, and hospital personnel continued to try and save his life, I continued to avoid the moment that was happening and my mind found solace in the fact that to him, I was more than a booty call with benefits. As Kevin's life and my affair with a married man that I loved came to a screeching Halt, I slowly walked down the hall in the same "invisible" manner that I arrived. Yet that walk was one that held on to a special recognition. As Kevin's life officially came to an end, I walked to the elevators that brought me to a place of answers, closed the doors, pushed the button for the lobby and as the tears formed and continued to fall, I found comfort in the saying, "Don't cry because it ended, find joy in the fact that it began."

Circle Complete

Two souls are known to unite either by love or by church and I wanted my soul to unite with Kevin's by both so I made my way to the hospital chapel. Nicole was still there. She was kneeling in the front pew praying to God out loud as if a higher volume in her voice would ensure her prayers would be heard and somehow overcome the situation and bring about change.

I sat in the last row of the chapel with my hands clasped together feeling dirty, sinful and trying to tune out with my prayers, my mother's voice which was repeating over and over in my head "What's done in the dark always comes to the light. You reap what you sow." I tried to fight the thoughts that suggested that because of our affair, Kevin sowed *Sin* and was reaping *Death*. I wanted God to see passed the sins Kevin and I had committed and spare his life.

I stayed in the chapel fighting with my prayers against my thoughts that God's wrath had been brought upon me and Kevin because of our sins. I was afraid that lightning would strike me in the chapel if I tried to ask for mercy while in the same room with an extended benefactor of my sin in the form of Nicole. But I tried. I was determined to stay there until Nichole, his wife, was given some news about his condition. After about thirty minutes of relentlessly praying in the same room with his wife, the doctor came in and delivered the news to Nicole.

Despite all the efforts of the doctors and nurses, Kevin Eckhart was pronounced dead at eleven, forty five a.m., September 14. Nicole let out a blood curdling scream when she heard the news and I left the chapel in the midst of her cries.

Kevin's birthday, entered as the password on my cell phone to retrieve the message that he was in the hospital was a precursor to the moment.

The stench of death in the hospital was a precursor to the moment.

The mistrial and the attack of Mr. Murphy, outside of the church was a precursor to the moment.

All of those things forecasted the impending storm which was brewing that would end our affair.

In shock and disbelief that Kevin was gone, I left the hospital and drove home on autopilot. I had cried so many tears, I had none left to fall. I repeated my Cognac poisoning from the night before. It would take being drunk in order for me to make it through the night. I was thankful for the drunken slumber once again. It allowed me to escape the reality of the issues at hand.

The next day, I mustered up enough sanity to call Judge McCormick and tell him that I had some serious family problems and would need an extended leave of absence. He didn't know what that meant exactly, but given the mistrial incident, he told me to take as much time as I needed to get myself together and he would hold my job while I did. After the call, I closed all the blinds in my house, ordered some Chinese food, put on the negligee that Kevin bought me and I didn't leave my house or answer my phones for four days. During that time I ate, drank, slept, drank, threw up, and drank some more. All in a solitary confinement that was self imposed.

September 18th ended my hibernation. It was the day of Kevin's funeral. I laid a black *Anne Klein* dress across my bed and stared at it for hours. I began to pace back and forth in front of my mourning ensemble, talking to it out loud, asking it questions of why Kevin had been taken away from me.

Of course the dress did not answer—like me, it was clueless.

Wanting nothing more than to crawl back into bed and sleep away my pain, I reminded myself that I couldn't let Kevin's funeral come and go without paying my respect. *Dirty little skeleton in the closet* that I was, I still had to see him laid to rest. So I threw up one more time and then got dressed.

Saint James Baptist Church was packed with those that knew Kevin personally, and with those that had seen the shooting at the museum on TV. The service was beautiful. I had never seen as many flowers in a church as I saw on that day. I would have personally given Nicole my acknowledgement of how well done the service had been put together, but I thought it better that my presence both at his funeral and in his life remain ambiguous to her. She knew nothing about me and I wanted her to be comfortable in her life as she knew it to be. In her time of grief, I owed her and the memory of him, that much.

Respect the dead.

There was no reason for me to sully Kevin's reputation or Nicole's vision of their life.

After the funeral, a fifty man motorcycle-police-motorcade, guided the funeral procession to the gravesite. Once there, the pastor said words over the coffin as it was lowered into the ground. I could see the pastor's lips moving, but his words did not register with me; my mind was elsewhere.

Someone told me once that you don't hear when death hits you. My mind couldn't help but question: Did Kevin hear death calling him? Was it silent—creeping up upon him like a thief in the night? I wanted to promise him that we would be united in his dreams. I wanted him to know that FINALLY, I knew he loved me and recognized that I was more than a booty call after all. I wanted him to hear my voice as I said that I was content and at peace with sharing my man; because having a piece of him was better than not having him at all.

As I ran my lips across the feeling of the taste of the words in my mouth, my mind's eyes were fixated on what was going on around me and the fact that Kevin's coffin was being lowered into the ground. I could see the pastor's lips moving, but his words did not register with me. My mind was focused on his coffin returning to the earth and my inability to accept the fact that he was gone. At that moment my knees buckled and I began to feel faint.

"Are you all right ma'am?"

There was that word again, I thought. And it is still dripping with sarcasm of wanting to replace it with the word "bitch."

I looked into the eyes of the rookie cop next to me and said, "No! I am not all right. Can you help me to my car?"

My head was light and my stomach began to do somersaults as the officer opened the door to my car for me.

"Nice plates ma'am. Are you sure you will be okay, because I would be happy to drive you home. You don't look well." The rookie seemed earnest in his concern.

"I'll be all right; I just needed to sit down." I replied, trying to muster a smile.

"Did you know Officer Eckhart well?" His question was surrounded by more than mere curiosity. He was being nosey.

With a cheesy grin, I answered, "I knew him in another space and time." I left my response at that.

The officer looked at me confused and then changed the subject offering again to take me home. I reassured him that I would be okay, and I started the engine on my SUV...4U2NV2 was on the road, and I took off. I made it all of about three blocks before I had to pull of to the side of the road to throw up again. As I did so, everything faded to black. When I came to, I was in the back of an ambulance. Apparently, my condition concerned the rookie and he decided to follow me as I left the funeral site.

I saw you pulled over, I saw you throw up, and then I saw you pass out. I didn't mean to invade your privacy ma'am, but you looked like you needed medical attention, so I called for assistance."

I smiled and for the first time, I noticed how handsome he was.

"What's your name rookie?'

"It's Dwayne Manson, but how did you know I was a rookie, ma'am?"

My smile grew in width and intensity. "Let's just say I know cops, and I can smell it on you Dwayne." I raised my hand to shake his and that's when I noticed for the first time, the IV that was attached to my arm. I knew then that Dwayne had been a savior to me.

After a momentary glance at the lines of sustenance attached to my left limb, I looked Officer Manson deep in the eyes.

"Rookie or not…Thank you for making sure I was okay. I appreciate that."

Dwayne's eyes closed for a moment as if he was building up his courage. He opened them and said, "It was both my duty and my pleasure. If you don't mind, I'd like to take you to lunch one day."

"How sweet," I thought as I noticed for the first time the greenish-brown hue of his eyes, the fresh military cut of his hair and the smell of masculinity about his person.

"Well, Officer Manson…lunches ALWAYS seem to get me in a lot of trouble, but since you were so kind to take care of me in my moment of need, let's do dinner instead."

He slid his business card into the palm of my hand.

"You rest now and call me later pretty lady."

He turned and left the ambulance.

Because my pressure was low and I had passed out, the paramedics insisted on taking me to the hospital despite my objections that I was okay. Once at the hospital, I was given a clean bill of health, but told that the doctor wanted to talk to me.

"I told ya." I said to the doctor. "I just had a little set back because of too much to drink for a couple of days. That coupled with the death of a friend, sent my body and mind into overdrive." I said the words more as a way to convince myself more than the doctor.

Dr. Christian Simmons reached in the drawer beneath him and said, "You're fine Ms. Thompson, but I like to give this to my patients as an aid for dramatical moments. You will need this."

It was a baby bottle with a bow and a ribbon that said, "It's a BABY, sex unknown."

My eyes froze upon his for what seemed like an eternity.

"Ms. Thompson? Are you all right? Do you understand what I am telling you? You are pregnant. You're going to have a baby."

I felt nothing but shock.

How could I be happy? Yet, How could I be sad?

Kevin and I hadn't used condoms because I was on the pill.

"How could this have happened?" I naively said.

"Well, apparently, you have been having sex, and with sex there's a fifty, fifty outcome of getting pregnant." His answer was glib in nature and we both caught the intended sarcasm of his statement.

"I'll need to set you up for prenatal care. Ms. Thompson...do you need or want me to notify anyone? The father maybe?"

"No, that won't be necessary, the father is dead."

That was the first time I used the word "dead" out loud in a sentence concerning Kevin.

A baby?

Kevin's baby!

How was I supposed to raise my dead lover's child alone?

God sure has a weird sense of humor, I thought to myself.

I left the doctor's office confused. Momma's words were ringing in my ears, yet again..."What's done in the dark, always comes to the light."

Kevin was gone.

His mistress, I was no more.

My life had changed

Mistress Memoirs

His seed I bore.

Good things come to an end
tainted ones end even faster
People enter our lives,
Kevin's purpose was more than lackluster
Because of my connection with him
I learned to
love myself more
Because of him, I was able to grow
And his child I now bore
My inner light now shines
I was his mistress for a reason
And because of our affair
Self-contentment is mine
if not for eternity
at least for a season.

Kahla

Postscript to an Affair

Some women become mistresses because they are gold diggers by nature; willing to sell their body to pay a bill, get some new Jordans for their child, or just because they need a manicure, a pedicure, or having their hair done and giving up their bodies to men so that the end justifies the means.

Some women become mistresses because they slip and fall before knowing what they are dealing with. They are bamboozled by men that conveniently forget to divulge the fact that they are married. By the time the men do offer that bit of information, the woman has already been hooked on the line.

Then there are the ones that are not gold diggers and have not been hoodwinked…the ones that made a decision—a conscious one, to be some man's woman on the side. They don't know WHY they do it, but they do. They do not recognize that they allowed themselves to be used because of self-esteem issues within themselves.

They do it.

They become mistresses.

Lorraine Elzia

They break up happy homes.

I never knew I would be a part of that THEY. But reality is....I've been there, done that; and I have the T-shirt, hurt feelings and broken heart to show for it.

Was it worth the pleasure?

Was it worth the pain?

Was it worth describing my thoughts

actions

and very existence

as insane

in the end Karma ruled

his Mistress I will always be

even if I fought the inevitable

he will always be a part of me

my world was typsey turvey

for my actions

I reap what I sow

wrong as he was to me

he touched my destiny

this I know

what Kevin and I tried to conceal

Karma soon revealed

and even in his death,

our eternal bond was sealed

I rubbed my growing belly

feeling sorrow

and happiness at the same time

I was once again where I started

Mistress Memoirs

in my big bed
alone
cold and lonely
with no man by my side
unlike the beginning
this time was not the same
for I had learned to love me
and self-acceptance I had gained.

Kahla

About the Author

Dynamic, Diverse and Deliciously full of flavor describe this Editor, Author, and Literary Artist. *Mistress Memoirs* is the debut novel for Lorraine Elzia, who has espoused the name *A Deeva*, and often writes under that pseudonym. She has always had an admiration for both the spoken and written word and has exercised that gregarious gift in various venues. That love affair of words, coupled with an addictive need to express herself, gave birth to a compulsion to write, which is a gift she is constantly nurturing. In 2005, she added the title "Author" to her lists of accomplishments with the publication of her first short story "Mommy and Santa" which was published in

"Chicken Soup for the Single Parent's Soul" and her poem, "I am a Woman" was a Letstalkhonestly.com contest winner. Those literary achievements were proceeded by a second publication in the *Chicken Soup* series in 2006 with the inclusion of her story, *"Letters of Love"* in the *Chicken Soup for the African American Woman's Soul Anthology*; inclusion in the *Katrina Anthology*, *Surfacing...Phenomenal Women on Passion, Politics & Purpose*, and a poem, *"Levitate"* in the *Gumbo for the Soul Anthology*. In 2007, Lorraine continued to strike while the literary fire was still hot with *"A Test of Faith"* in the *Triumph of My Soul Anthology* and she is a contributing author in the upcoming second *Gumbo for the Soul Anthology*, with inclusion of her poem *"Am I My Brother's Keeper."* Lorraine is co-owner of an editing company: Eve's Literary Services, contributing editor of the *"Gumbo for the Soul"* series; and co-moderator of *Essentially Women*, a writing group for African American women. She is from Austin, Texas, by way of Motown (Detroit, Michigan) and it is her desire that through the written word delivered in different genres, she will be able to inspire and motivate others to see the beauty that resides within all people.

Visit Lorraine online at www.LorraineElzia.com.

Titles from Peace In The Storm Publishing

Serving Justice by Jacqueline Moore
The Ministry of Motherhood by Cheryl Donovan
Mistress Memoirs by Lorraine Elzia
A Whisper to a Scream by Elissa Gabrielle
Hiding in the Shadows by Claudia Brown Mosley
Suicide Diaries by Ebonee Monique
The Baker's Dozen by S.D. Denny
Holy Seduction by Jessica A. Robinson
Good to the Last Drop by Elissa Gabrielle
Point of No Return by Elissa Gabrielle
Do You Still Do? by Cheryl Lacey Donovan

THE TRIUMPH SERIES
The Triumph of My Soul
The Soul of a Man: A Triumph of My Soul Anthology
The Breakthrough: A Triumph of My Soul Anthology

VISIT US ON THE WEB
www.PeaceInTheStormPublishing.com

Mistress Memoirs

Ordering Information

Yes! Please send me _____ copies of
Lorraine Elzia's *Mistress Memoirs.*

Please include $15.00 plus $2.00 shipping/handling for the
first book and $1.00 for each additional book.

Send my book(s) to:

Name:_____

Address:_____

City, State, Zip:_____

Telephone:_____

Email:_____

Would you like to receive emails from
Peace In The Storm Publishing?
____Yes   _____No

Peace In The Storm Publishing, LLC.
Attn: Book Orders
P.O. Box 1152
Pocono Summit, PA 18346

VISIT US ON THE WEB
www.PeaceInTheStormPublishing.com

LaVergne, TN USA
10 May 2010
182152LV00002B/7/P